Writer's Quarry

Story Ideas for Authors

Ben Sheldon

authorHOUSE®

AuthorHouse™
1663 Liberty Drive
Bloomington, IN 47403
www.authorhouse.com
Phone: 1 (800) 839-8640

Published by AuthorHouse 10/21/2016

ISBN: 978-1-5246-4455-0 (sc)
ISBN: 978-1-5246-4456-7 (hc)
ISBN: 978-1-5246-4454-3 (e)

Library of Congress Control Number: 2016917341

Print information available on the last page.

Is a collection of original creative ideas for writers looking for fresh ideas to start a new story or novel.

Hell on Earth

A leader (Hal Godwin) of some religious fanatics gets a vision from God, to create a Hell On Earth, for heretics. He locates a secret spot in the jungles of, say, New Guinea. Hell's design would be as close to the Bible's description of Eternal Hell. With his followers, they create a network to transport blasphemes to their hell, and drop them in there on the raging flames.

The Writer will use imagination and creativity to manage the details.

Holy Hallucinations

Temporal lobe epilepsy causes visions and hallucination.

A neurologist rides a time machine, and travels to see Jesus, Saint Constantine, Saint Bernadette, and others who had divine visions, to check for himself, whether they suffered that malady, causing hallucinations.

Air Force I Hijacked

With the President in it, is hijacked to a hostile country.

Work out the details of destination, negotiations, ransom, etc.

Midas and Saddam

Midas touch turned it into gold. Saddam turned it into feces.

One day the two meet. Work out the detail of the encounter, who wins, and how. What is the visible aftermath of the struggle.

World War II On Parallel Planet

Combatant roles are reversed. The Japanese nuke Pittsburgh, PA. The Germans burn Birmingham, England, just as Dresden was.

Work out the morality, justifications, etc.

Murder Ala Cart

Man murders a person, cooks him. When investigators arrive, he feeds them his murderous cuisine.

Murder At Space Station

Shady astronaut kills colleague and sets him sailing into space, on way back from Mars landing. He sneaks back rocks to sell for a high price in the black market.

Origin of Hell

Before there was Hell, God summoned Gabriel, and asked him to design Hell for Him. In the Holy Blue Prints, He wanted to see the recommended temperature, duration (in millennia), method of firing (gas or electric, atomic (e.g. the sun) or?). May consult with the burners of Joan of Arc and witches of Salem, oil refineries, and/or big-city fire departments.

Borrowed Fingerprints

Criminal obtains fingerprints of an innocent person, puts them on a thin film. He grafts the film onto plastic gloves. Wearing those gloves, the criminal commits his planned murder, leaving the innocent man's finger prints in the scene of the crime.

How Extraterrestrials Took Over Earth

They engulfed planet Earth with numbing neurological waves, or temporarily disabling gas, then took over the whole planet. After using up all the human flesh for protein, here and for supplies at their barren planet, the creatures leave for the next victim planet.

Planet of Hell; Planet of Heaven

Astronauts, lost in Space, land on a strange planet, with Earth-like atmosphere. They discover it to be the actual Hell; same or another planet where they find the real Heaven. The writers will use their imagination as to what they see; whether it is based on the Bible, or something original that the Scribes missed.

Exploring the planet they come across people they knew on Earth. The good ones were in "Heaven"; the bad ones in Hell.

Xmas in July

Activist starts movement to shift Xmas from December to July, the good season. Santa gets wind of it and vehemently opposes the move. Gets support of the Saints, Jesus(?), etc. along the lines of "Miracle on 34th St.".

Sleep Talk Evidence

Suspect in a crime nearly gets away with it, until someone sneaks in a recorder into suspect's bedroom and records his dream talk while he/she is asleep. Clues, names and hints are then pursued.

Garbled talk is replayed backwards, to show intelligible talk for leads.

Steam Event

A unique king in an unusual kingdom, allows subjects to let off steam, on a certain calendar day, once every 10 years. A worker will cuss his boss and call him names. No violence. The king will show up in a square and make himself available for cussing out, & letting off steam. And so on.

The Prankster

Incorrigible, he/she does any or all of the following:

1. Drugs cats and dogs, and sneaks them in bags, etc. into a side room of a plush hotel, then puts them out in an obscure corner. When they come-to, the pets run into the event or banquet rooms. The dogs howl at the guests, while the cats run away with the steaks and other meats. Some dogs pull at the elegant long dresses of the upper crust ladies.
2. At a grand reception, Royal Gala, etc., the prankster carefully places matches (or flammable match heads) some distance inside cigarettes, and substitutes them for the guest cigarettes at the high class event. As the grand guest or host puffs at his/her cigarette, till it reaches the match head. Suddenly, the cigarette's front end lights up in a flame. The writer will use imagination and story context as to how everyone reacts.
3. At a noisy next door party, the prankster sneaks in with powdered sleeping pills, and furtively sprinkles the powder on the edibles of the energetic noisy guests, before they return from their hopping, dancing or love corners. Prankster then goes back to bed. After a while, he/she notices that the neighbors are nicely quiet, and goes to sleep.

Underground Utopia

An idealist billionaire buys an island, and builds an underground city in the island, with the aim of a crimeless utopia. He then hand picks the residents of the city from all over the world, with strict character criteria.

The city functions and prospers, until something happens. The writer will use his/her imagination, as to where to go from here.

Psychoanalyzing a country

America, before the 1960's was uptight like in a straight jacket. It was nerve wracking for the country, as a cultural unit. It got tighter and tighter, until America had a nervous breakdown. She did not care what she looked like after that. That is when the hippie movement began. Looks and fashion were no longer a factor in the life of America, as a unit. The hippies lived like unkempt devil-may-care lives, while the rest of the country looked on nonchalantly, like recovering breakdown patients, aggravated by assassinations of JFK and MLK, and senseless self destruction—further manifestations of country's nervous breakdown.

Author can develop this theme, in parallel with a relative or loved one, who had gone through a nervous breakdown. How that compares with a country, as a unit, recovering from a nervous breakdown.

Catula and Dogula

Dragula is unable to find a human to provide him with an opportunity to suck his/her blood. The desperate vampire settles for a cat or dog to suck its blood as a last resort.

1. The cat turns into Catula becomes a vampire cat, and sucks the blood of its sleeping masters, birds, and any animal or prey. Catula may also jump on top large animals, like cows, elephants, etc. to suck their blood, and turn them into vampires.
2. Dogula does similar things, with some variations of its potential to create vampire creatures, from their masters, to the animals they contact.

The author will choose his/her own specific location and circumstances.

Airport Thief

Thieving passenger furtively exchanges tags with a luggage of a prosperous passenger, whom he/she knows contains valuable contents. The victim ends up with the crook's luggage at his own destination, while the thief ends up with the valuable luggage at the criminal's city of disembarkation.

The author can incorporate this into their own theme, or build a separate story around it.

The Syringe Man

A maniac intent on having revenge on cops, or society, walks around with a covered secret syringe or hypodermic needle. He injects drugs, poison, or such harmful fluids into drink cartons, etc. and walks off. He/she can do that in shops, at parties, political rallies, depending on the story to be developed. He/she could also inject fluids into eggs, fruits, ets.

The author can choose his/her own story or theme, to fit this maniac into the story. He/she could be a disgruntled doctor, orderly or plain criminal.

Firebug with Silent Timer

Pyromaniac uses candle as a timer. He/she places candle on top of the bare end of the fuse wire. Candle size (height and thickness) will depend on the estimated time for the explosion. It is determined by the length of time the firebug/arsonist needs to establish an alibi, for when the fire is triggered as the candle expires. The length of the fuse wire will depend on how far the explosion would be from the candle initiator.

Anti-matter Meteorite

Rare anti-matter meteorite hits Earth. It neutralizes an equivalent amount of Earth matter into a giant explosion, with no trace of any matter left. The huge crater created by the enormous explosion leaves no trace of any visible matter to study by scientists. Implications are huge. A future anti-matter meteorite, or stray planet the size of Earth or greater, could neutralize all of Earth into a massive explosion, with no trace of Planet Earth left anywhere in space.

Steam Hammer Murder

In old style steam heaters, when turned on from cold, condensation causes hammering noise. Killer takes advantage of this noise, to shoot his victim.

Author can use this as a basis for a murder, or incorporate it in the existing story.

Sell Oneself

Social crusader seeks to change the law to make it legal for himself to sell himself as an indentured slave for a specified amount of money. His/her new status gives him a good amount of funding, and he gets taken care of with room and board, which his/her "owners" must provide, by the new law of indenture, or labeled 'slavery' by opponents.

The writer can develop the theme in different directions: moral, immoral, religious, etc.

Terminal Man's New Fate

A sick man, call him Joe, is given a few month to live. He has had a controversial life with many enemies. Joe embarks on a revenge spree, against his tormenters. Bodies of victims show up all over. For a long time Joe is above suspicion, being terminally ill.

Mysteriously, Joe's malady goes into remission. Meanwhile, the evidence of himself being the murderer mounts, and he is arrested.

The author of this idea can develop it in many different directions. Options go like this:

1. Prosecutors do not know that Joe's illness is in remission; so Joe gets a favorable treatment he does not deserve;
2. Lawmen know Joe's malady is in remission, and is sentenced to death, now by fellow humans, instead of the disease—poetic justice;
3. Other ways that fit the writer's imagination.

Small Accident Mushrooms

A normally insignificant incident, leads to international catastrophe. E.g. a rat eats into a wire at NORAD, or other highly secured place. This time, the critical cut wire, or similar matter, sends a nuclear missile to Moscow, or a destination that would fit into the writer's plot.

OR the cut wire could initiate a chain reaction of events that might lead to an electric blackout in the North East, or some other region of the US, or Canada, depending on the writer's story.

Mafia and Monastery

Outlying isolated monastery is taken over by a Mafia gang. They kill the monks, and use the monastery for drug smuggling. Being isolated, no one learns about the crime

The writer can make this a main theme, or incorporate it into his own outline.

Wish of a Dying Gay Man

His last wish is to have all his ex-lovers rounded up, and seated around his deathbed, to reminisce about old times, and how the ailing man's life evolved from one lover to the next. They will remember those who died of aids and other maladies. Add in a lot happy and unusual memories.

The author can include their own characters and experiences to suit their evolving plots.

Unholy Apocalypse

A cabal of atheists, who are brilliant scientists and engineers, hatch a giant plot to nuke the most holy places of the major religions: e.g. The Vatican, Jerusalem, Mecca, etc. They believe that all the world's ills emanate from major religions.

The author can add his own holders of certain beliefs and religions.

Iraq Veteran Rents from Iraqi American

Angry Iraqi American (IA) must rent an apartment to a US military man, who happens to be a veteran of the Iraq war. The IA has had relatives killed by US bombs, in Iraq. Deep down, his hatred and anger continues to mount, to the point of plotting to harm the US military man.

The author can develop this premise into any direction he/she chooses, with this "captive victim" in mind.

Hypodermic Needle Blackmail

Blackmailer threatens fruit and vegetable shops (or supermarkets), and demands that they wire money to a certain immune foreign bank account, OR he/she would inject poisonous fluids into their fruits and or vegetables, using a hypodermic needle. Process would be very discreet, with a cover over the injecting needle, to avoid store cameras.

Author can adapt the idea to their specific localities, whether a small rural shop, or a large supermarket in a big city. He/she could live in a foreign country and have an accomplice in the US or other country as a location.

Pilot's Plot

Pilot of a passenger airplane locks the cockpit, when copilot goes to the bathroom. He then calls the tower that the plane is hijacked, and will be blown up, unless a certain person "known to the hijacker" is released from prison.

The writer can use his/her imagination as to who the jailbird is. He/she could be a gay lover, a relative, etc., depending on the theme of the story.

Holography Kid

An electronic whiz kid learns ins and outs of holography, to play tricks on his family and friends.

The author will develop the story into unexpected channels, creating unusual situations. Some could cause problems for parents, teachers, etc. Others could propel the kid to fame and stardom.

Tele-transport Machine

A genius invents a tele-transport machine and experiments with it. Persons, animals, plants, etc. travel at the speed of light to any destination the inventor configures in the software. At Departure Chamber, the transportee has his/her atomic inventory digitized, then the atoms are transmitted to the intended destination, where the software reassembles the atoms into the person that was at the start of travel.

The author can take many different paths:

1. scientific research;
2. Planned migration of humans to another planet, if Earth is anticipating a huge, annihilating asteroid, headed towards our planet.
3. Prankish scientist who uses his/her invention to play tricks on friends, relatives.
4. Military personnel use it to tele-transport personnel, equipment, etc.

Cyanide Asteroid

An asteroid consisting substantially of cyanide, deadly material, and or gas, is heading towards Earth. The noxious substances, rather than the impact, will be the great killing machine.

The author can approach the story:

1. As a scientific project to divert the asteroid; or
2. Decide it will hit Earth and perhaps wipe out humanity, and figure ways of survival; or
3. Asteroid inevitably impacts Earth. The author figures out if any life still exists, considering the type of poisonous air that engulfs our planet.

Iraqi and US Vet in America

Healthy Iraqi has avoided conflicts of his native country, and now lives happily in an apartment building in an American city. His neighbor happens to be an amputee and US veteran of the Iraq war.

The author can develop the theme in different directions. E.g.:

1. The Iraqi can feel terrible guilt that he did not sacrifice for his country; he let a "foreign" young man ruin his life, to liberate Iraq for him, while he enjoys life peacefully in America;
2. A hidden tension permeates the lives of the Iraqi, and the US veteran of the Iraq war. The vet could suffer PTSD, and have nightmares that his Iraqi neighbor is preparing an I.E.D (improvised explosive device). If a car backfires, the vet jumps out of bed, slides into his wheelchair, grabs a weapon, and heads for the Iraqi's apartment.
3. The Iraqi can take it upon himself to care for the US veteran, to mitigate his feelings of guilt.

Clones of War

In a futuristic world with much conflict, and depleted family members, the government allows each family to create a one clone, to send to war and sacrifice in conflicts, in lieu of a real family member.

The writer can approach it in different directions:

1. In case of a defective clone, a family is required to provide a real family member to be sent into harms way. To avoid that, a black market develops for others' clones, illegally sold for needed money;
2. Some clones turn out to be mentally deficient, aggressive, or difficult to trainable. The government would return them, for real family members;
3. Clones returning from war, secretly gang up together to take over the system that sent them to a devastating war.
4. Author's imagination into other aspects.

The Plot for Temple Mount

Israel secretly masters the fight electronics of Iran's aviation, from airplanes to rocketry. Israel then provokes Iran to retaliate, by striking at an Iranian site, on some excuse. Iran then seeks revenge, by sending rockets, with powerful explosives to Tel Aviv. Israeli electronic experts then send signals to the Iranian rockets, and redirect them to hit and totally destroy the Muslim Dome of the Rock and al-Aqsa Mosque, to clear the way for building the Holy Temple, as mandated by the Bible.

The author can develop this in different ways:

1. At the UN, Israel will argue that Iran destroyed the Islamic holy sites. So the site cannot be that important to Islam, hence it will commence building the Holy Temple;
2. The Iranian action creates a great chasm in the Muslim world between the Sunnis, lead by Saudi Arabia, and the Shiites, lead by Iran. The horrific action could lead a widespread war between the Sunnis and Shiites. While they fight it out, Israel builds the Holy Temple. By the time the Muslims settle the conflict, they face the fait accompli of the new Holy Temple on the site of the destroyed holy Islamic structures.
3. Islamic world could smell a rat, and suspect Israel, and start an all out war against Israel.

The writer could develop the direction of the conflict.

Transplant

An Arab boy needs a heart transplant. The only heart available is from a Jewish victim of a car accident. The Arab family is split on having their son living with the heart of person from those who have transplanted his people and have been oppressing them.

The author will develop it and decide which member is for it, and which against, reflecting the old and new mentalities clashing, leading to the writer's tailor-made resolution.

USA and Power on Trial

Advanced and righteous beings from another planet take over planet Earth. They extent their interplanetary court to Earth, and try the powerful country who had gotten away with grave crimes, because no one could challenge their power.

First case on the agenda is Hiroshima. The author will set up his/her case for and against indicting the USA.

Second case: Nagasaki. Similarly developed by the writer.

Third case: Saudi Arabia. Their power from oil economics, has made them immune from justice. The author will arrange the case in the Interplanetary Court. Issues to be treated could be oppressive Wahabism, and the fanaticism emanating from that.

Fourth Case: Israel and the Palestinian conflict, and whether immune USA has also extended its immunity to protect Israel, after establishing a state at the expense of an indigenous population, who had lived there for 2000 years.

Fourth Case: Whether Native Americans are entitled to take their country back. Whether those who followed Columbus are entitled to take someone else's land.

The author will develop each case, wherein the verdicts could go either way, with the neutral Inter Planetary Court.

The writer could add his/her own tailor made case.

Miss Corporations Pageant

Participating companies and corporations pick their most beautiful executives, and have them compete in a pageant.

The writer will develop the details of his/her own story line, with all the conflicts, intrigues, etc.

Autobiography of a Bear (or Lion, or Cat, or Dog, etc.)

The animal tells its own story from birth (with mom filling in) to the end.

The author will pick the animal he/she is familiar with, and develop a path of life for the animal, to be related by the animal.

Invest in desert Island

Tycoon buys a desert island cheaply, because of lack of water. He then brings in desalination facilities all over. He subdivides the island, and sells to select type of people.

Author will use his/her imagination as to what kind of people, what type of society the tycoon wants to establish in this faraway desert island.

Historical Gambles

a) Those that did not pay off: e.g. Gallipoli;
b) Those that paid off: e.g. Korea's Inchon landing.

Author can pick "a" or "b", or both, and develop into disastrous consequences for one, and/or victorious ending for the other.

It can have fictionalized characters, with a human side to it;

Or it can be developed as nonfiction, from the writer's favorite angle.

Chestnuts and bullets in the fire:

Fourth of July, or Christmas time: practical joker, throws chestnuts in the fire, then a bunch of live bullets, which explode and take off every which way.

Author will develop the theme according to his own contrived story:

a) whether a bullet hits anyone—who, where, & what happens;
b) or if a bullet grazes a pet, etc.

The randomness of the flying bullets lends themselves to endless possibilities.

(Note: a young guy told me that his dad actually threw some live bullets into the fireplace; but in this actual case no one got hurt from flying bullets.)

My Two Lives

Life one: I live to survive, doing mostly things I do not like, but must do to survive.

Life two: I do only things I like.

In the end, the two lives are compared. Life 2, would be the could've, would've of Life 1. State of minds are compared, and so happiness levels, and whether it was worth it.

The author will pick the type of personality he/she is familiar with, and plots the life plan accordingly.

Undocumented Columbus

A fictional America, wherein lives an advanced native population, in various independent nations, with strict border controls. They achieved this after years of conflict and research into weaponry.

Columbus arrives onshore, and is met by a native coastal patrol. When he fails to produce permits and/or ID papers, he is taken into custody.

The author will develop this according to his own plot, as:

1. Comedy, with all the irony of white men barging in on a sovereign native nation, ignoring their laws and norms. The reader will compare it to the plight of undocumented immigrants to the US, and relish the poetic justice involved;

2. Serious Fiction, wherein the writer can turn the tables on the whites who took over a country that belonged to someone else—the natives, this time with no impunity.

Abortion Murder

Abortion doctor is killed by a fanatic, and goes on the lam. A fundamentalist doctor tries to protect him, by helping the killer to cross dress and live as a woman, till the heat is off his crime. After a while, the fugitive realizes he is actually a woman inside a man's body. The protective doctor conducts a sex change for the fugitive, along with a uterus transplant. In time the killer meets a man who gets romantically involved with the transgender fugitive, who gets pregnant. The killer is not ready to bring up a child, and seeks abortion. The closest and most convenient one, is where the doctor "he" killed used to operate.

The writer will develop the idea in the direction that suits his imagination and temperament. It could be:

1. A serious treatment, with a moral;
2. Or a comedy involving irony of ironies.

Insured Politician:

Creative insurance company comes up with an insurance plan on certain politicians.

How the plan works: the voter client will pay a premium that a certain politician he decides to vote for will carry out the important promise (or promises) he makes, during his/her campaign. If the politician does not pursue his avowed promise, the insurance company will compensate the voter client, according to payment table.

The premiums will be figured based on each promising politician's record of reliability.

The author can treat it as a comedy, or a novel approach to reliability of a politician.

Flowers for Saddam

Takeoff on Mel Brooks': "The Producers". A Sunni Iraqi American writes a book glorifying Saddam and his achievements, ignoring his criminal record. He shows how wrong the two Bush presidents and Britain's Blair were, as shown by subsequent impartial assessments and the rise of ISIS.

The author can write a comedy, nonfiction, or a mixture of both.

1. As a comedy, the writer can have the book peddled as a movie potential. He approaches different types of movie producers with varied views about Saddam. The reactions can be humorous to violent:

a) like when he unknowingly offers it to a producer, who is a veteran of the Iraq war, perhaps a relative of a contractor who was burnt alive in his car in Fallujah or Ramadi. The producer goes to get his shotgun, as the book's author takes off with his life; OR, the Quarry writer may develop it into his/her own theme.
b) Or he approaches a producer, whose Kurdish American wife saw genocide committed by Saddam. There is a comedic conflict between the producer and his wife about the production. The Quarry author can develop it into his/her own theme.

Seniors Rule

Futuristic times, wherein health breakthroughs enable people to extend their average lifespan to 200 years. The planet is overwhelmed with a population that it cannot sustain, leading to severe birth control. The result, the majority seniors rule the land. Being retired, they extract high taxes from the few young working class folks. This friction can lead to all kinds of conflict.

The author will develop a theme from this premise.

SUICIDE BOOK:

A how-to book for committing suicide.

The author can take one of two approaches:

1. A comic treatment on unusual and untenable ways for one to commit suicide;
2. More serious book on how to commit suicide safely, without suffering or injury to others; how to settle financial and other matters before the decisive act. The legalities of this approach will be explored.

Valuable Lessons I did not learn at school (or college)

Most of us have learned great lessons from our friends, relatives, or even strangers.

The writer will recall some of these lessons, how he acquired them, from whom, and what results he/she got out of them in life. Why the lessons were superior than anything learnt at school (or college).

Astral Object heads for Earth

The writer can choose from various approaches:

1. Futuristic world, where space travel is common for the wealthy who can afford it. The wealth gap will create two classes of survivors:
    a) The rich who can escape the planet to a predetermined spot, where they have vacationed before. They will bide their time, to return in safer times, to explore habitable spots in a devastated planet;
    b) The poor who must hunker down and find a way to survive the catastrophe. The author will develop ways for them to survive (or not).

2. Current world wherein the scientists and engineers find a way to:
    a) Deflect the astral object, depending on the size, speed and distance from Earth;
    b) Destroy the astral object with atomic power, or whatever way the writer chooses.

Counter Kidnapping

A criminal kidnaps a person dear to a wealthy person, who has eyes and ears in the community. He digs up crucial information about the kidnapper, and who is the dearest person to him. The rich guy gets hold of his mob contact, and makes a secret agreement to counter kidnap the person dearest to the kidnapper.

The writer now has two parallel subplots going:

1. Official, legal attempt at recovery of the kidnapped; and
2. Unofficial mob-assisted way to return the loved one, wherein the two kidnapped persons will be exchanged, without paying a ransom.

The author will work out the details as to which method will succeed, how and why

The Great Wall of Mexico

Futuristic USA builds a wall along the length of the border with Mexico, with watchtowers and barbed wires. Various Mexican groups dug tunnels all across the border to bypass the wall. The groups could be smugglers of people or drugs.

The writer will pick a group and build a story around their operation, and the cat-and-mouse "games" they pursue to avoid being foiled by the US authorities.

Head Exchange

Husband and wife conduct scientific experiments, similar to the ones in the science fiction movie: "The Fly" (with Vincent Price). Except, here, something different goes wrong—the wife ends up with the husbands head, while the husband gets the wife's head. Other variations:

1. Father and son exchange heads; 2. The son clandestinely dabbles in this type of science, in the presence of his pet (cat, dog, bird, etc.), and end up exchanging heads (or other body parts, like legs, paws, etc.).

The author will select his/her own characters, and plot the story accordingly.

Character Flaw

A person with a small character flaw in normal times, is thrust into a dire situation, like a plane crash, requiring abnormal interactions with survivors--the flawed character being one of them.

The author will select a male or female protagonist, with a specific flaw in mind. The writer will show the protagonist in normal times, with his/her flaw not a serious impediment in everyday life. The protagonist will then be flung into an unusual situation, which will magnify the character's flaw, to its limit, as he/she tries to handle the situation with colleagues, passengers, etc.

The flaw could be mild depression, vertigo, claustrophobia, stuttering, fear of certain animals, etc.

God Comes Down

God descends to Earth as a human, opens an office on Main Streets, with secretaries, paper work and computers, and operates like a corporation. He is assisted by angels, like Gabriel, who print out prayer books, receive and guide miracle seekers. They advise God as to what liar to be struck by lightning and where, as displayed in the computer screen on a map produced through Godquest. The screen also shows all praying subjects all over the world, and marked by the angels as to whose prayer to answer, after displaying their secret life on the computer screen.

Red flashing arrows indicate God's decision on an imminent flood or earthquake orders, on a selected sinful community. To save a rare good individual, like a devout woman, Gabriel will get her on the phone: "This is God speaking. Go to high ground, to avoid my flood." The flustered lady shakily replies: "Please, Mr. God, can you give a little extra time?" She also sucks up to God by telling Him about this organization which is spreading rumors that "God is dead". Gabriel recommends to God that she consult with Jesus Christ Superstar about this.

The author can develop the story line in many directions: as 1) A comedy; 2) A moral parable, etc.

Citizenship for Sale

In a dire futuristic Earth, the Government is bankrupt. Foreign countries are in a worse situation. To raise desperately needed funds, to run the government, a new law is passed, wherein any citizen who is desperate for money, to survive, may sell his citizenship to a foreigner, and temporarily stay here on a visitor's visa. After its expiration, he must move to the country, whose national had bought out his citizenship. Meanwhile, the government has collected a good chunk of the transaction money as citizenship transfer tax, or CTT.

The author may pursue the overall theme in many different directions. He/she can layout a background as to why and how this dreadful situation befell this country, and/or the rest of the Globe. It could be a resistant bug that spread quickly, causing widespread devastation; or atomic conflict, etc.

Human Flesh for Alien Planet

Astronauts stumble on a stark alien planet, with strange-looking creatures raising humans for their protein nourishment. They are advanced enough to canvas other planets for essential foods that their planet was no longer able to produce. The alien planet had similar facilities for their weird looking inhabitants. They had stores and butcher shops, stocked mainly with human meat. It is packaged and displayed the way beef is presented on Earth for human consumption.

How the aliens got the humans to breed and raise for their protein consumption, throws light on the strange sightings by Earth denizens over many years.

The writer may emphasize different aspects:

1) The trip details by Earth's astronauts, and how they stumble on this strange, food-starve planet;
2) Aliens abduct Earth denizens. Our advanced society finds out and tracks the aliens return trip to find out their unsavory plans;
3) Find out how this alien society lives and conducts its business.

Random Bio

Pick a person at random, and write his/her biography.

The author may choose his/her own type of "random" person, who might fall in the category of:

1) Hobo; or 2) Bill collector; or 3) Delivery man; or 4) Postal worker; or 5) Teacher, etc.

The idea is that every non-descript person, whom we see in everyday life, may have a fascinating life story to tell. The writer may tell it in Fiction or Non-Fiction form.

The Gravity Aliens

Science Fiction story, about highly advanced aliens, who are able to temporarily alter Earth's gravity, before they invade our planet. They can increase or decrease the gravity up to or down to any level they choose. The two ultimate scenarios are:

1) Zero Earth Gravity, wherein the armed military personnel have difficulty staying put in their camouflaged hiding places, as they float up, without gravity to hold them down. By the time Earth people get wised up to it, it may be too late;
2) Double or triple gravity is imposed by the aliens, in which case the military personnel, weighing double, or triple their weight get stuck to the ground, as the aliens safely land on our planet.

The writer can pursue his/her own variations of this general plot. He/she can pick the zero-gravity theme, or the high gravity theme. The author may also create his/her own story as to why the aliens are invading, and whether or not Earth prevails and how.

Explosive TV

FBI or CIA embeds an explosive device inside the TV set of an enemy, terrorist, etc. When the outlaw accesses a certain dangerous and forbidden channel, the device explodes, eliminating the enemy of the state.

The author can create a theme, or build a story around that.

Cracked Engine Blocks

Pranksters or vengeful criminals in a cold winter climate, drain the radiators of targeted cars, then fill them with tap water alone, without antifreeze. At night, the freezing temperatures crack a lot of engine blocks.

The author may choose to pursue:

1) The Prankster theme, and build a story around it; OR
2) The criminal story, wherein the culprit gets even with a winning lawyer, etc. by causing engine damage to his/her automobile.

Embezzlement Payoff

Airline accountant embezzles, say, half a million, from his employer. He then arranges a hijacking, or kidnapping, and secures half a million dollars, intended to pay off the embezzled amount. The upshot of the of the scheme is that the embezzler clears half a million dollars for himself.

The writer will pick a theme, and build a story around this embezzlement process, with all the potholes and pitfalls. The author can throw in a crooked wife or girlfriend accomplice; OR work with a willing disgruntled employee to perpetrate the complicated scheme.

Underage Murderer

An apparent 18 year old guy commits aggravated first degree murder, for which he receives the death sentence. Just before execution, his mother comes across an old authentic birth certificate, which proves her son was underage when he committed the murder. By prevailing law, he could not be executed.

The writer can develop the story line, involving the killer, his mother, lawyer, and all the related people and events, with a lot of emotional content.

Borrowed King

Two mythical kingdoms, Molo and Baldi, lived side by side, in 400 AD, say. After a long conflict, with each king trying to conquer and absorb his lucrative neighbor's territory, they decided to end the mutual wars. But the sneaky intrigues continued. King of Molo, secretly produced a baby, with a distinct marking tattooed on its foot. The baby was then clandestinely and very carefully placed at the doorstep of the king of Baldi, who did not have an heir to his throne. Thinking the baby was abandoned, the Baldi courtiers took the infant in, and showed it to the king, who immediately adopted the baby as his son and heir to the throne.

In time the king of Baldi died, and his grown, adopted son was crowned king. That is when the reigning king of Molo emerged and let it be known that the new king of Baldi was his real and true son, who was now ruling on behalf of his biologic father.

The author can follow a story line that would suit his/her abilities and interests.

Secret Driver

A woman (Martha, let's say) who never drove a car, secretly learns to drive, in pursuit of a diabolical plan. She hates her husband, (call him Ralph),who has a million dollar life insurance policy, with Martha as the beneficiary. One day, Ralph gets run over by a car, in a dark alley, with no witnesses around. No one suspects Martha, for ostensibly, she cannot drive any vehicle.

The writer can draw up a plot based on that. He/she would figure out how and where Martha secretly learned to drive; how she planned to murder Ralph, without arousing suspicions. It would involve how and where to temporarily get control of a car, to pursue her murderous scheme.

The author will then pursue the post-murder denouement in a choice of possibilities:

1. Martha gets away with it, as reward for her longtime suffering;
2. She can get blackmailed by someone, who claims he/she has evidence to indict Martha. The blackmailer could be a nosey neighbor, or the out-of-town driving teacher.
3. The writer may have his/her own plot to suit their experience and local.

Goodwill Club

Group of creative and compassionate people form a club to cheer up persons who are ugly, and feel unwanted. In one instance, one of them, GC1, say, will approach an aloof woman at a party, dance etc. and invite her to his table with another club member, or GC2, sitting there. The GC (Goodwill Club) guys will act as Hollywood producers, and put on an accent. GC1 will look at the lady's unattractive face, and, turning to GC2, will say: "We could use her in our new movie." GC2 will reply: "Oh, you mean 'The Loves of Jacqueline?' "Yes, her face has good bone straakcher (structure, in the chosen accent)".

In the end the club members leave her with a renewed sense of self worth.

The author can follow a theme that suits him/her, with their own selected characters and scenes.

Guilt and Credit Allocation

In a company, passing the buck, or claiming undeserved credit is a chronic problem. So, management forms the "Guilt and Credit Allocation Department". Employees are encouraged to pursue their talents to the utmost, and not to be hindered by mistakes that has adverse effects on the company and colleagues. If something goes wrong and others have been disadvantaged, the culprit will not blame it on others or find excuses, but will refer the matter to the "Guilt and Credit Allocation Department". All affected will meet here, and divide any blame based on what happened to whom.

Similarly, if someone has come up with an original idea, and someone else claims credit for it, the aggrieved will request a meeting of GCA Department, to allocate or subdivide credit.

The writer may develop the theme to suit her/his specific plans and area of expertise.

God Retires

God decides to go out of business. He advertises in religious magazines and websites, offering Hell and Heaven for sale. Hell will be cheap, but will require a lot of fuel to keep the fires going. Heaven is priced at a million prayers down and 10,000 prayers a month for a thousand years.

The author can vary on this basic idea, and follow a comic theme, or a hell and fire story.

Innocent Getaway Car

Two men planning a bank robbery, find a Unique scheme to use a third party's auto, as a getaway car. They drive their more expensive car, looking for a teenager, or naïve guy, with a cheap automobile. The criminals "casually" meet this car owner at his auto, and discuss a straight swap. Of course, the cheap-car owner agrees with no hesitation. However, to make sure the inexpensive vehicle runs good, the criminals want to take it for a ride, by themselves, leaving their expensive car with the simple guy, as security. They put an empty suitcase in that car.

The criminals drive to a bank they had planned to rob, do their deed, and get away in this auto of the innocent folks. They give it back to their owner, claiming that it is too much for them to give up, as the two quickly climb into their car, with suitcase full of loot, and disappear.

The writer will fill in his/her own plot, as to what happens to the innocent owner of the cheap getaway car. How the law catches up with the criminals.

Ten-dollar Cadillac

This is based on a true story that happened a few years ago. Here, a man had a wife, and a mistress on the side. When the husband died, he left a will, requiring that his new Cadillac, to be sold by the estate's trustee, his wife, and the proceeds be given to his mistress.

The wife advertised the Cadillac for sale at a price of $10. Thinking it was a joke, or some hoax, few people called. One trusting soul pursued the matter and purchased the new Cadillac for $10.

The true story ends here.

An author can take it from here and build his theme and twist to this episode:

The mistress gets wind of the wife's scheme, and persuades a friend to purchase the Cadillac for $10, and then give to the mistress, who hands him/her a reasonable reward for the auto acquisition.

The writer can come up with other variations, and conflicts.

Back from the Dead

A man who had died and been buried, one day shows up at his home, and claims he went to Heaven, and met Jesus, the apostles, and talked to God. That he was sent back to let the skeptics know that he brought evidence that what he was told, on Earth, about Heaven and Jesus was true.

He is questioned in a press conference, and answers all questions as a convincing eyewitness.

The author can take it from here, into themes of:

1) Conspiracy; 2) Mental illness; 3) True revelation, etc.

Serial Killer Team

Two or more serial killers form a team to do their nefarious deeds, but confuse the investigators.

For instance, Killer 1 will do his criminal acts. When he is arrested on suspicion of committing rare type of murders, Killer 2 will do similar murders, to mislead law enforcement personnel that they have the wrong man in custody for these types of unique murders. Hence killer 1 would be released. If and when Killer 2 is held in custody on suspicion of murders, Killer 3 will go out and do the same kind of very unusual type of killings, to confuse the cops and have Killer 2 released, as per their prior agreement.

The writer can do variations on that theme, perhaps specifying the murders in more detail, and what makes them unique. He/she may assume only 2 killers, or a group of criminals forming a pact on serial murders and/ other crimes.

Suicide Dispensation

Devout catholic has terminal illness, and is in constant excruciating pain. He travels to the Vatican to seek dispensation from the Pope to end his life.

The author will explore the state of mind of the sick man, his relations with his folks, and their reaction when he decides to a dispensation from the Pope. A lot of soul searching and much tension will be involved, for the writer to navigate logic and religion.

Time Machine on Select Visits

A current day ardent reporter learns the ins and outs of a Time Machine from a scientist interviewee. He can even operate the time machine almost as well as the scientist. The reporter always had wondered what it would be like to interview certain historical figures who fascinated him.

One day the reporter "hijacks", or takes off with the Time Machine, and travels in time to visit and interview, say, Abraham Lincoln, Jesus, Andrew Jackson about the Trail of Tears, et.

The writer has great latitude to plot an itinerary for the reporter, and how and where he gets back.

Alien Donors

Aliens, disguised as humans, donate their sperm everywhere. This is how they propagate their kind on Planet Earth, to eventually take over our planet, and use it as a safe haven from their dying planet.

The writer will pursue this there and vary the story around that, with options like:

1) Earth humans do not find out until it is too late: or
2) They find out, by accident, early enough to conduct counter measures. This would include some kind of dragnet to locate the sperms and destroy as much as possible;
3) The new alien progeny is spreading out and themselves donating sperm to further propagate.

Bulletproof Skin

Genetic research combine crocodile and turtle genes onto human genes to produce humans with bullet proof skins. In IQ and everything else, they are like normal human beings. The military and police forces clamor to recruit these new bulletproof humans.

The author can follow different plots, like:

1) The ethical line, wherein a new class of humans may face discrimination and boycott, out of fear:
2) The military and police forces encourage the "production" of these shielded humans for defense and law enforcement;
3) Foreign powers engaging in large scale spying and cyber hacking to get the top secret formula for producing these bulletproof human beings.

Cereal Killer

A man kills his victims in the morning, by sneaking into their kitchen and putting poison into their milk, which is subsequently poured onto their cornflakes and kills them—hence the name: Cereal Killer.

The writer can follow a comic approach to the plot; or a more serious story.

Arctic Dinosaur Egg

A dinosaur egg is found by a scientist in the arctic, as global warming caused layers of ice to fall off. The scientist immediately preserves the egg. Later he incubates the egg for several months, until it hatches into a baby dinosaur.

The author can choose from several story lines:

1) Raising the dinosaur, to become a huge pet; or
2) Grows up into uncontrollable menace; or
3) The writer's own protagonist in his/her own original story.

Beetle Conspiracy

True story: Pine beetle in Montana, a few years ago, forced the fast chopping down of pine trees.

Take off on this event: A developer near a national forest needs easy inexpensive lumber. But he is far from the legitimate sources of lumber, which gets very expensive, by the time it is hauled to his place of business. To get the easy lumber from the protected forest, he clandestinely seeks to find a tree beetle to introduce into the nearby national forest, to force instant tree cutting. This would provide a quick and cheap supply of lumber for the developer's projects.

The Author Can Choose from Several Themes

1) Developer's quest for the beetle, takes him to universities, scientific organizations, while disguising his sinister intentions;
2) He has the beetle. Now he has to find the right areas to introduce the beetle in, without arousing suspicion onto the developer's evil deed;
3) Developer has limited number of beetles, and decides to breed more, before embarking on his criminal enterprise;

Murder Memorial

Mother of a murdered guy crusades to create a memorial to murdered victims, similar to the Vietnam memorial. It would list the names of all the murdered persons. A day would be set aside every year to remember all those murdered.

The writer can pursue several themes:

1) The obstacles encountered by the activist mom, and all the unpleasant comparisons she hears from critics, comparing her goal with a "sacred" Vietnam memorial. She counters, that her dead child's life and soul is just as "holy".
2) Vietnam veterans create great obstacles for the mother;
3) The crusading mother eventually succeeds, and attends the inauguration of the Murder Memorial

Devil's Office

The Devil sets up an office in town and recruits assistants, to help bring over to him, the atheists, the antichrist and those forsaken by God. He conducts rallies, and even runs for election.

The author can work the psychology and details of this version of the Devil's operation in some interesting directions:

1) The writer can place the Devil in a town at Zip Code 96666 and a toll free phone number of 866-606-6666. He will invoke his constitutional right to freedom of religion, or non-religion;
2) The Devil's assistants may attend Christian mass and rituals, to spot the disillusioned, in the congregation. This could lead to arguments and perhaps altercation with the "Faithful";
3) He can play hide and seek with God, who is seeking his GPS location, to send a bolt of lightning; OR
4) Writer's choice of his/her own theme and treatment.

Mafia's Paid Pipers

The Mafia is able to locate and recruit pied pipers in different towns. They use them to blackmail the townspeople. In this mythical setting, a fable is hijacked by the Mob.

The author has options:

1) Can concentrate on the children of the wealthy;
2) Blackmail a whole town;
3) Play cat and mouse with the Federal Government seeking to put them out of business.

Magic Aerosol Can

A kid finds an aerosol can on the beach. He presses the aerosol spray button and a genie appears, and thanks the boy for releasing him from this can. He tells the kid that he can perform one wish for him, since the genie was in the can only 100 years. The youth thinks hard about this only wish.

The writer uses his/her imagination to come up with a theme that fits that one wish.

Alien Insects

Creatures from Outer Space select a location on Planet Earth to land on, but must clear it of humans first. These aliens send tiny guided objects that look and act like insects, or robo-insects, that home in on the humans in the picked area. They bite on the necks of people and kill them in seconds.

The author will pursue the story from there, as to what these alien creatures are up to, and how they proceed to take over the marked location.

Roaming Spirit

A man has the power to inject his spirit into other creatures, like humans, birds, insects, etc. He can then see everything his spirit host can see and feel and explores what is going on inside the body and brain of this person or animal. He can even charge for this service in important situations like:

1) The new wife of a billionaire: is she really in love with him, or is she just after his wealth?
2) The partner in a company: is he honest, or has he been embezzling?
3) The bird in the cage: is it really happy when it sings?

And so on, depending on what the author has picked for a story plot.

Parallel Lives

Two persons meet and it is love at first sight.

The story is about each one a few years back, and how they lived their everyday lives. Where did they, and what did they do every day and night. How these two persons, who had never met before, travel from their two totally different backgrounds, find their way to that one spot, where they met and fell in love. Was it a convention? Did they meet fighting a war? Was one of them a jailer, and the other a new inmate? The possibilities are many.

Psychic Conspiracy

A guy in a group is secretly picked for a psychic experiment. His colleagues go on a silence conspiracy, and give him looks, like weird and perhaps crazy. The study goes on to find out how far can press someone's mind before he breaks down and goes crazy.

The writer has the option of pursuing many possibilities:

1) The subject eventually breaks down and goes crazy;
2) One colleague confides in the subject guy and tells him what they are doing to him. The writer can write about the disrupted experiment, and how the flawed results are treated;
3) Or other possibilities.

Electronic Painting

Artist/engineer invents an electronic canvas, with many wires and fine points inside, all connected to a keyboard. His paintings are of the same quality as the regular canvas paintings. Also, it is more flexible. He fine-tunes, adds or subtracts without messy paint all around. He patents it as "Paintless Painter".

But he is not accepted as an artist in the art community.

The engineer/artist copies his electronic painting on a normal cloth canvas, as an original painting. He is now called a fraud.

The author will use this theme to pursue the conflicts and jealousies in the Art World.

Too Peaceful

Futuristic world, where all major problems have been solved, and everyone makes a secure living, with full healthcare from cradle to grave.

Human beings remain conflict oriented. A group of Detergent Activists promote Spotless, and call themselves "Cleanites". A fiercely counter party promotes Ajax soap, and are known as the Ajaxonites. Eventually each forms two parties named by those names. They run candidates for elections. The Cleanites nominate Mr. Clean to run against Al Jaxon of the Ajaxionites. Mr. Clean promises to nationalize all Laundromats and provide free cleaning for all citizens. Al Jaxon claims that their opponent's philosophy is tantamount to socialism; but he will provide free soap for every household.

The author can follow different paths:

1) Comic path of two serious parties who adopt policies that appear trivial to a still troubled world;
2) Serious path to show how the humans are designed for conflict, no matter how much of their major problems they ultimately solve.

Learning Robot

A scientist builds a Robot that continuously learns and improves its creativity and manual dexterity. Eventually the robot creates another Robot in its image, and achieves at the same creative level. The new Robots replicate themselves, until their numbers are enough to take over a wide area of a lightly populated state. From there the Robot numbers increase exponentially, till there are enough of them to take over the state where they started.

The writer will then develop the story from here:

1) The central government gets alarmed, and tries to contain this menace;
2) The Robots outthink and outmaneuver humans at every stage: OR
3) Other ideas that the author could develop and pursue.

Life's Compartments

Psychological novel or story based on the premise that a person starting out in life does not progress in a straight line. Instead, he/she move up (or down) from one compartment to another. Within each compartment, she/he progresses to the limits of the "walled" compartment. After that, it is a leap into the next compartment, where progress is made within the wall of this new compartment, to its "walled" limits.

The author will come up with characters similar to those she/he is familiar with in real life, and a plot drawn from real life, that may have happened to a member of their family, a friend, etc.

Germany & Japan Win WWII

In a parallel world, Germany and Japan won World War II. Two separate sets of war-crime trials are pursued by victorious Germans in Europe, and the triumphant Japanese forces in the East.

German Trials

Trial E (in Europe): After the German V-E & A (Victory in Europe & America), the Nazi High Command sets up Trial E, in the Tower of London, for war crimes done in Europe against the German Fatherland. A major focus will be on those responsible for burning down the historic city of Dresden. High profile politician in German custody would be hauled into court, to face burnt witnesses and others from Dresden and other places involved in the fire and trying to put out the conflagration.

The writer could use her/his imagination as how the Germans won World War II, whether by top secret atomic weapon, devastating germ warfare, etc.

Author using this premise, can produce his own bunch of characters, from Churchill to Hitler, etc. and provide an imaginative plot. Perhaps executing some "guilty" ones, by symbolically beheading them in the Tower of London. Some imaginative strings may be pulled here, about Nazi techniques.

Trial A (in America): The Germans could set up war crime trials in Washington D.C., Philadelphia, or other symbolically significant city, to mock the freedom and democracy professed by the losing allies.

The author may create some story line wherein the Germans unexpectedly introduce a horrendous weapon on the Americans, to speed up the end of World War II. The writer will use imagination as to who will be picked for the trial, like some famous or colorful war personalities from President to generals, etc., maybe in a mirror image of the Nuremberg trials, or a unique German trial, or borrowed from their Teutonic era.

Japanese Trials

These could be coordinated with the Germans, or conducted separately, to reflect the unique damage done to them in Hiroshima and Nagasaki. If done separately, the Japanese could do their trials in Hawaii, like perhaps at Pearl Harbor.

The writer can create his/her own plot and WWII characters, and how they will respond to the devastation caused at Hiroshima and Nagasaki.

The American Inquisition

A politically correct party wins a landslide victory in the US, and sets up an American Inquisition, similar to the Spanish Inquisition. Anyone using words like "nigger", "kike", "pedophile Mohammad", would be subjected to intense interrogation, including the newly legalized water-boarding. They must produce all their influential contacts.

The author will be creative as to the story and where it leads the reader. For instance, those labeled anti-Semites, racists, or blasphemers of other religions, must be registered with the police, wherever they live. They may be required to domicile a specified distance from a synagogue, mosque or black neighborhood—along the lines of child molesters.

Language Pills

A creative doctor invents pills that, if ingested, would immediately cause the user to speak in an accent as specified in the pill's specs for that language.

The author's imagination may attribute the patented pill to the unique research of a doctor, perhaps a neurosurgeon, who specializes in the brain zone, where language is used, by different nationalities, and how the nerves respond to different accents. The imaginative doctor could create nationality-specific pills, producing the specific accent selected by the pill taker, for a movie roll, or whatever.

Characters and plot may adopt this theme, or a variation of it, to suit the writer's talent and experience.

Dictator's Term Limitation

A dictator takes over a poor country and causes endless suffering for a highly religious population. They prayed and prayed, with no positive results in their oppressed situation. The most popular movie there, was "It's a Wonderful Life," wherein an angel was sent to save the good-hearted citizen, who was mired in deep problems and contemplated suicide.

This time, God sent his angel to "term-limit" the dictator, and terminate the people's suffering.

The author will have leeway as to how the despotic ruler will be approached, and the sort of threatening punishment, which would be heaped on him, if the despot did not relent, and halt the suffering of these poor, richly religious population.

The Pill and the Bullet

Health conscious guy lives in a crime-ridden neighborhood. He takes all the precautions to avoid predictable ills. One thing he could not guard against is the unpredictable bullet from a gunfight.

The writer can provide two parallel plots:

1. The protagonist, leading a healthy life, to ensure a long life;
2. Armed gang, with their nefarious activities.

The two plots interact, in a gang war not far from the Protagonist gymnasium, where he is exercising. A stray bullet hits him, and he is dead, despite all his plans for a long life.

The author may vary the plots to fit her/his own experiences or story line he/she prefers.

Twin Agents

Two identical twins, A and B, end up spying on opposite sides (X and Y) of a conflict. Twin A spies for side X, while twin B spies for side Y.

The writer has many choices to develop an exciting plot. For instance:

1. Side X may suspect twin A may be a double agent; while:
2. Side Y may not suspect twin B to be a double agent; or
3. Side Y may suspect twin B to be a double agent.

The author has a great deal of leeway to figure a great plot for the story.

Untimely Deaths

A guy is affected by the death of a famous person he used to think about when the person was alive. Such well known personality could include: Vince Lombardi, Walt Disney, JFK, Martha Mitchell, Sadat, LBJ, Hubert Humphrey, or others, that would interest the writer.

The novel's protagonist would visit the grave of the dead person selected by the author. At the grave the protagonist would conjure up his/her imagination, and bring the selected personality to life, and deal with him, to finish the business the protagonist wanted him to do when alive.

The writer can fit the plot into his life and experience, or what he perceived in the news.

Modern Trial of Jesus

When Jesus was arrested and was ready for trial, by chance a time machine from Today had just arrived in the vicinity. When Pontius Pilot found out, he ordered all evidence taken to Today, and examined, and results brought back by the Time Machine. Some evidence would be checked for DNA, in saliva and blood. Other evidence would include finger prints from the Holy Grail, etc. Forensic analysis would include a psychological profile.

The writer can come up with her/his own set of evidentiary material, whether on the serious or humorous side, depending how the plot path is chosen.

American Untouchables

Author, from India's untouchable caste, visits America, and comes across US's own caste system.

It ranges from the homeless, ghetto blacks, elderly, gays, etc.

The writer may select a plot to include one or more of US untouchables, and have the Indian protagonist pursue the line in comparing it to Indian untouchables. Other characters could be included to further pursue the similarities or differences. The plot could veer into romantic, intellectual or other area's depending on the author's propensities.

Santa Claus, the Vampire

A vampire loves the young fresh blood of children. So he becomes a Santa Claus. Christmas time, kids flock to him. When no one is looking, he sucks their blood from the neck or elsewhere. Santa then places a gift ornament around the child's neck, covering the tiny bite mark.

The author can follow the life of one kid, as he grows up to be a vampire himself. Characters will include the kid's parents, friends or relatives, as the child's strange behavior unfolds, and they try to figure out the son's new unfathomable ways. They might take him to a child psychologist, etc.

Ill Mom and 3 sons

It is war time, and three brothers rotate on going to war--always leaving one son behind to care for the bedridden mother. They agree on a fixed period of time for the one assigned to care for the mother. After the period is up, the next sibling returns from war, to care for Mom, while the current care-giving brother goes to war.

One of them gets killed, and the other two rotate for mother's care. A second son gets killed, leaving the third one in permanent care of his mom.

The writer can choose a plot to create conflict between the brothers, as who should stay or go to war, depending on the situations, whether any of them have love affairs, married, or have kids; or whether any one is injured—lightly or seriously.

Protector of the Holy Places

Saudi Arabia is the protector of the Muslim holy places such as Mecca and Medina. However, the US is the protector of Saudi Arabia. Is the US is then the protector of the Muslim holy places?

This premise can be the basis of a story line that creates great conflict and argument at college or in Arab streets. The writer may inject intrigue, public unrest or even murder, depending on the direction of the plot he/she would prefer to pursue.

Created conflict could be limited to a family; or it could lead to riots within a country; or even a regional war, pursuant to the author's plot.

Heart of the Enemy

An Arab man needs a heart transplant. The saved heart of a dead Jew can prolong his life. But the deep Arab-Jewish bloody and deadly conflicts going back for decades, complicates the decision making for the very ill Arab guy.

The author will invent a story line wherein friends and relatives try to persuade the sick Arab, to take the Jewish heart. Others who have suffered from Israeli violence, urge him not to accept the heart, which would make him a "partial Jew", with all the suffering they had caused the Arabs.

The plot chosen by the writer, could be a philosophical overview of the Middle East conflict, and the human aspects; that, ultimately all humans are basically the same, no matter how they are classified by themselves, or others.

Christian "Caliphate"

Captured ISIS leader is taken to International Criminal Court, in The Hague, for crimes against humanity, in the process of reviving a Muslim Caliphate.

The trial will bring out all the conflicts and atrocities and present them on the human level, away from the bloody battlefield.

The story's plot may bring up arguments for both sides. ISIS leader can argue that the Muslim Caliphate is no different from the Catholic "Caliphate", with "Caliph" Pope being elected by the cardinals, who are equivalent to the Shoura members, who should have elected every Caliph, as decreed by Prophet Muhammad. The author can vary the story line to suit his favorite characters and story line.

Life-support Conflict

A violent confrontation between two persons, say man and wife, leads to the wife to be badly injured and is on life support. If she dies, the husband may be charged with murder. If the wife lives, the charge cannot be murder.

The victim's mother and father want the life support stopped, and the wife declared dead. The husband is vehemently against this decision, which could reclassify the case as murder. Hence, the husband does everything he can to keep the life supports.

The writer can be creative as to this deadly conflict and which way it will, go: whether the husband's way or the path the wife's parents want. Additional conflicts, including murder, could be injected into the plot.

Two Gangs Rob Same Bank

Two independent groups, by chance, rob the same bank at the same time.

The author will have a field day with a plot of many intriguing possibilities. She/he can follow a comedic story line, or a serious one, depending on how the writer wants to develop the events. The two gangs could have different motivations. For instance, in "Dog Day Afternoon", the motive was to obtain money for a sex change operation for the robber's lover. The second gang may have a more serious reason to rob the bank.

The motivations and the conflicts, plus the injection of cops, would make a most fascinating tale, laced with a myriad paths the writer can create.

Vampire King

The monarch of a kingdom is exposed to a situation, wherein the king turns into a vampire. He keeps it a secret for a while. During that, he picks individuals from his kingdom to visit his palace. The unwary citizen feels honored to go to the royal chamber. Here, the vampire king sucks the blood from the naïve subject.

The plot can follow many paths, depending on the author's preferences. Initially, the monarch will easily dispose of the dead victims. As they increase in numbers, court personnel may suspect foul play.

A second option would be that the king's victims do not die, but transform into vampires too. Perhaps there will be enough new vampires created, that the whole realm would turn into a Vampire Kingdom, with a whole new set of story line options.

Black Planet

Astronauts come across an Earth-like planet, which is populated by white inhabitants as well as black people. However, here, the black community rules the planet through their own laws, and elected black representatives. In addition, they use the whites as slaves, who have far fewer rights than their black masters.

The story can be developed in a number of ways. For instance, the life of the enslaved whites may be similar to the Old South plantation life, but now the blacks are masters. The writer may chose similar cruelty or injustice, or have the blacks behaving more humanely.

The writer could inject forbidden areas in intermarriage, rules for slave trading, etc. Many other variations are possible, whether as a commentary on the Earth situation, or new creative differences.

Dart and the Royal Horse

Animal welfare activist is back from Africa, and crusades for human treatment of animals in the West. These include circus animals as well as the Royal horses, pulling the Queen's carriage to open Parliament, which he picks for his ultimate publicity.

On Parliament's inauguration day, the activist picks a choice spot in the procession route. He has his tranquilizer dart ready, but covered in a bag. When the Queen's carriage approaches, he shoots a dart into a lead horse (& perhaps a second one, time permitting, into the second leading horse). He quietly slips out, as the poison from the dart takes effect, and the front horse (or horses)fall down in the middle of the procession, creating great chaos, and a security nightmare for the Queen's protectors.

The writer can choose a variation of this idea, in the context of:

a) Assassination attempt; b) Against a dictator, in a different country; c) A circus, to highlight animal cruelty there; d) Horse racing: shoot a dart at the lead horse at Churchill Downs, etc.; e) Bullfighting: tranquilize the bull with a poison dart, before the animal is cruelly killed.

Rape Baby

A woman (call her Jane) is raped and gets pregnant, with an unwanted baby. She is not able to get an abortion. The baby is delivered in the hospital, in a room Jane is sharing with another woman (named Irma, say), who is expecting her baby too. At the right moment, Irma is asleep, Jane exchanges her infant with that of her roommate, Irma.

The author has a choice of developing this theme into a number of different directions:

a) Jane's new baby could have been infected with Zika virus, from her biological mother, Irma. The plot gets complicated by Jane's dilemma of whether to give back Irma's baby, in exchange for her "rape" offspring; or making the best of the new situation;
b) Dispose of Irma's baby, with 2 consequences: 1. Jane get caught in a murder situation, with its own plot line; 2. Jane gets away with murder, but later hankers to get back her child from Irma. This would make for another theme for the story.

Invisible Spray

A chemist develops a chemical, which when sprayed on flesh, renders it invisible. This would apply to humans, animals, birds, fish, etc. The duration of invisibility may vary, depending on the author's plot.

This basic idea lends itself to be pursued in a variety of story-line directions. They could include:

a) Person, who escapes police, sprays himself and temporarily disappears; b) Pranks on friends or relatives, wherein the joker sprays their pet, who temporarily vanishes, while still barking or meowing. c) Spy or detective can spray himself and walk into a room, where adversaries are discussing secret plans.

Complication in the plot can happen, when the duration of invisibility becomes uncertain, due to the nature of the chemical. This would lead to sudden reappearance of a detective (or spy) at the wrong time. The author will deal with that to heighten tensions, and maximize reader interest.

Roommate's Lottery Ticket

A roommate (named Sam, let's say) had bought a ticket. It was lying on the kitchen table, while he was away at work. John, the guy sharing the apartment with Sam, finds out that John's ticket is not a winner, but Sam's ticket has won 50 million dollars. Sam does not know that. The writer may assume that Sam knows his ticker numbers or not (as with Quick Picks), depending on the author's chosen story line.

In one plot, John could cash out Sam's ticket and disappear. When Sam finds out his winning numbers, he pursues John high and low. The writer has a choice of:

a) Sam finding John, and follow a story line accordingly; OR
b) Sam does not find John, but, while in pursuit, he encounters other factors, gurus, etc. and learns a more valuable lesson about life and money.

While in Orbit

Astronauts, in a space capsule, have been on a long term endurance test to last five years. In the meantime the international political climate on Earth deteriorated, resulting in an accidental nuclear strike by one Great Power, followed by nuclear retaliation by the other big power, who was attacked, with much loss of life.

The astronauts see the mushroom clouds sprouting all over planet Earth, as communications with the space capsule abruptly halt.

These incredulous spacemen confer in the orbiting capsule, as to what course of action to take. They decide to wait it out as long as possible, till radioactive dust settles. Then they would select the safest spot on Earth to land after reentry from space.

The writer may pick protagonists as:

a) US and Russian astronauts in the space capsule, sent up when the two powers were collaborating in this endeavor;
b) All-American crew in the capsule, with their quirks and anxieties; or
c) All-Russian spacemen, orbiting the Earth on an extended biological study.

The author could explore in more detail as to how the conflict started. Possibilities may include:

1. A rogue nation, or stateless group acquires an atomic weapon like purchasing from another country, like North Korea--with a grudge against a super power; they would provide means of delivery too. The roguish party would target a large population, and launch their atomic warhead from a spot that would incriminate the other big power;

2. A disgruntled, suicidal employee of one power, finds out the secret code and sends out an atomic missile to strike the adversarial superpower;
3. Conspiratorial group in Russia, say, give up on the system ever going democratic and decide to cause suicidal destruction, by sending an atomic warhead to hit an out-of-the-way, unprotected area, with substantial population.

Nobody Wants the Presidency

Futuristic USA, wherein prior presidential candidates have been grilled, insulted and badgered to the point that no one would seek the presidency at the next election. Without candidates there can be no President.

The writer will explore this story line, and the ensuing constitutional crisis, and how the author will pursue the problem to a solution or intensified crisis.

At the Pearly Gates

A long line of people we know are trying to get in.

The writer can see a former Pope arguing with Saint Pete, who is asking some tough questions. One could overhear some of Apostle Peter's questions, like: "Why did you start the Crusade Wars, in the name of the Prince of Peace (Jesus)?" Another question overheard: "The Messiah preached that if you get struck on the left cheek, you turn the right cheek to him. Why was every Jew and Muslim slaughtered when your crusader fighters entered Jerusalem?" This Pope was asked to wait, while Peter interrogated a warrior Pope, then asked another Pope about the sale of indulgences, as Martin Luther waited in line behind him.

The author may select other persons trying to enter through the Pearly Gates. They could be relatives or friends, who have done bad things, but thought that they were the gift of God on Earth. Saint Pete could question some about persecution of gays, whom the Lord created that way. Why were they questioning the Lord's creation?

In another situation, the clergy who blessed soldiers going to war: why would they do that in the name of the Prince of Peace, Jesus.

Or other themes the author may wish to explore under this general banner.

Holy Braille

A humorous story on the premise that Jesus had failing eyesight in his last days on Earth. The Apostles invented a "touch" language, similar to Braille, to enable the Messiah to write His parables in this improvised "Braille". One parchment was produced, in "Braille", as Jesus spoke one parable. It is believed that the Templars got hold of the Parchment, which disappeared in France. After that there ensued a race after the Holy "Braille".

The writer may have variations on this humorous theme. Or produce a more somber believable alternative.

DNA of Jesus

A scientist investigating the Shroud of Turin and other religious artifacts, comes across a relic from which he extracted what he believed to be the DNA of Jesus. The scientist uses that to produce clones of Jesus. He then donates these clones to any city or community that wants one to improve the morals of their people. Eventually, most cities and communities end up having their own Jesus clone.

The writer may develop this story line further, to where Jesus cities or groups improve morally; OR these groups get into conflicts as to who has the real Jesus. On the international level, a country may use its military, headed by their Jesus, to conquer another country, headed by their own Jesus clone. The writer has many options with plot and character drawn from his own town and experience.

King Arthur in Connecticut

The Connecticut Yankee manages to get King Arthur visit his state. He drives the king around in his car, with the radio playing concerts and other music that impresses King Arthur. The king is taken to horseracing, flown in an airplane, and a hot air balloon, as well as a roller coaster.

When King Arthur returns to Camelot, he orders what he saw in Connecticut, to be copied in his kingdom. To start with, the king orders a side carriage attached to his royal one. The attached carriage housed a band from the best musicians, to play while the king traveled in the main royal carriage. This would the equivalent to the car radio in the auto he traveled in while in Connecticut. The author will describe the problems in Camelot, when the side-by-side carriages enter a narrow road.

Another "invention" King Arthur wanted in Camelot, was the hot air balloon. The writer could have a field day with the problems the king will encounter with this balloon, whether King Arthur rides in it or not. The balloon could drift away in a gust of wind, with the king landing in hostile territory or strange lands. Court intrigue may cause bad guy to be sent away in the troubled balloon, never to be seen again.

Ballgame Prankster:

A disgruntled baseball fan, fills the bat of an opponent with explosives, for revenge in beating his favorite team in the World Series, the previous year. Upon hitting the ball from the pitcher, the bat explodes, with the extent of the damage developed in the writer's plot line and story.

A similar theme could be used on a football fan. With prior "inflate gate", it could develop into a totally different type of "gate".

The writer may pick a specific team he/she is familiar with and put in real or fictional ball players.

The Inheritance Plot:

An aging tycoon wants to write his will, but is not sure whom he should leave how much of his fortune.

The billionaire conspires with his doctor to pass some false health information to his offspring and relatives, and candidate for the inheritance. The doctor tells all those expecting to inherit, that "Big Daddy" is ill, and has limited time to live; that the tycoon does not know it.

The story ling will unfold, showing the intrigue and plots of one group, and the loyalty of another group. All this makes it clear to the rich will writer who should get what, as well as who will get zero, for all the reasons "Big Daddy" will detail in the will.

Dearest Clones

A scientist clones his Mom and Dad, before they die. So he will always have them around, in clones, even after the parents die.

In the story line, friend or neighbors beg the biologist to clone their parents or dear ones. The author will decide if such cloning is legal or not. In each case, what would the scientist do for these desperate acquaintances. If the clones are illegal, what do they do to hide it, if there is an investigation. The writer may even profile the clone and whether he/she is happy to be an extension of the lives of others, or would they prefer to lead their independent lives elsewhere.

The author may tell the story in first person, as happening in his family, and whether he/she can reproduce the original emotional atmosphere, when the real loved ones were alive.

Secret Camera

Hotel (or motel) owner installs a secret camera in the ceiling, not for security reasons, but to satisfy his personal quirks. He could be:

a) A voyeur, to record guests having sex in his hotel room; or

b) He may be collecting damaging information against an opponent; or

c) The hotel owner could be engaging in blackmail, to supplement his income, stave off bankruptcy, and keep the hotel in business.

Unexpected things may come into record. For instance:

1. Sex partner could murder a guest, who might be the owner's wife, relative, etc.
2. The murderer may be known to the hotel owner, with the writer pursuing that plot line; or
3. The killer could be a total unknown to the owner, to follow a different story line;
4. If the blackmail angle is chosen, the evidence will be used differently.

Ejacula

About a dracula who will suck the blood of his victims, then must have sex with them, till he ejaculates bloody semen, to show he had enough blood.

The author has option for many different story lines, depending on the quirkiness of this vampire. It could indicate a special weakness, wherein a potential victim could get at the blood sucker.

The Live Glove

A glove has its own independent will. Whoever wears it, does not have control over his/her hand that is covered by this magic glove.

The author may choose one of several story lines:

a) Sinister tendencies could be inherent in the glove. The wearer may be lead into unwanted actions—some even tragic; or
b) It may be a benevolent glove, helping the wearer avoid unpleasant, or even tragic consequences;
c) The glove could do good things for benevolent persons; or negative happenings to nasty people.

The writer may have his/her own chosen plot for the story.

California After the Atomic War

After the atomic war, California's population is reduced to a quarter of its prewar number. When everything settles down, and the air is clean again, suddenly the remaining residents realize that California has gone back to where it was seventy years before. There were small isolated towns between San Jose and San Francisco, with miles of uninhabited land in between, just like the Old Days. The area code for the Bay Area went back to "415", discarding "510", "925", etc. Internet towers have been devastated and there is no longer internet, just like the old days.

To many nostalgic old folks, the good old days had come back.

The writer could pick a storyline that emphasizes this nostalgia for the old "small town" days.

The old Mexican bracero fruit picking program could come back.

The younger folks go to drive-in movies again.

Age for Sale

A scientist in a foreign country discovers a "gene enhancer" drug/chemical that will increase a person's age by many years—the number of increased years depends on which drug one buys. The price of the drug goes up, depending on how many additional years the drug buyer wants to add to his/her age. The scientist lives in a secret place, so no country or force can find him to persecute or prosecute him for any trumped up charges.

The "gene enhancer" drug can increase one's age from 20 to 300 years—the latter being very costly.

The writer could pursue this story line on many levels:

a) The scientist could have a genuine breakthrough medicine. There will be no end of customers wanting to "buy" substantial extra years to add to their lives. Author's plot will tell us how some of these people, with bundles of money in hand, can find the scientist, to purchase this amazing life-prolonging magic medicine;
b) Medical "inventor" is rumored to be a charlatan, and the country with the most "victims" who had purchased the drug, is clamoring to find him and bring him to justice. The writer will create characters, who will pursue this goal, with perhaps a surprise ending.
c) The magic drug had been invented in Shangri La, in the rugged mountains of a Tibet-like country, and as difficult to reach, as in the classic movie, "Lost Horizon", based on James Hilton's novel. Except, here the drug inventor has set up shop and sells the medicine, which is priced as per number of years the buyer wants to live—up to 300 years.

The writer may choose any of these story lines, and pursue the story based on his/her own characters and their incentives to advance the story. The ending could be a surprise of the type the author will have creatively put together.

Incompatible Heart

About a person of principle, who needs a heart transplant--with the organ available from another person of a totally unacceptable persuasion. Options for the author include:

a) A priest desperately needs the heart of a donor, to survive and continue God's work in his ministry. Bur the only available organ is from an atheist, who never repented or converted. The writer will get into the mind of the priest as he mulls this dilemma, and whether God would approve. What will his family and congregation think? Will the priest put them all to a vote, to accept or reject the atheist's heart. Or:
b) An ailing atheist must have a new heart to survive. However the only available heart is that of a priest, who had died in an accident. The atheist must solve his dilemma of having to live with a priest's heart, which had been asked for Jesus to come into. Would that violate his principles? Is it better to die, than adhere to his atheistic principles? Or:
c) A Palestinian must have a heart transplant, but can only get that of a dead Jew. What will his refugee family think about living, with part of him being Jewish—perhaps from a family who had caused them to suffer as refugees. Or:
d) A sick Jew needing a new heart, after losing it in conflict with Palestinians. Would he want to survive with only a Palestinian heart being available. Could he walk around with part of him belonging to those who had caused his affliction?

The author may pick anyone of these plots, or one from his experience, pausing a similar dilemma for his/her character.

Pompeii's Gay Community

Archeologists are puzzled by a Pompeii discovery. In one of the houses, in the basement were the bones of a very large group of young males huddled together. It appeared that the place was a popular meeting place for Roman gays, around the time of the giant Vesuvius eruption.

This fictional theme could be expanded on, to create a gay life in Pompeii at the time the volcano that destroyed this Roman city. The author could be inventive, and put in material gleaned from actual historical gay characters found in Roman history, and their way of life. A made-up gay Roman emperor could be thrown into the mix of the writer's characters. A gay brigade of Roman soldiers my distinguish themselves in battle, then have a gay bacchanal, after the successful fight, with captured enemy youths.

What's in a Name?

A movement in the United Nations would ban the use of misleading names. For instance, the Democratic Republic of the Congo (DRC) is summoned to the UN, to explain the logic of its name, before the world body will allow the use of its name on an international scale. The Congo representative must justify each word in the country's name:

1. Democratic: Why use this word, when the country was never democratic. The pervasive rape of women by government soldiers and officials are well known, with no recourse to justice for the victims, in this so called "Democratic" state;
2. Republic: when the public has no voice in electing the government, why call the country a Republic.

The author will create characters, so that a Congolese representative will present a defense for his country, to enable it to use the DRC name internationally. He will bring the example of East Germany, after the Second World War wherein this communist dictatorship called itself "The German Democratic Republic". The Congo official will argue that there was nothing democratic about the despotic Erich Honecker, who ruled the country for years. It was not Republic, because the public did not elect the East German leaders.

The author will get the Congolese to answer the UN representatives as to why a democratic republic could be the world's greatest rape center.

Theory of Conflict

A dedicated student has a theory that all conflicts, including world wars, start from small differences, and build up. Protagonist finds that each side grossly underestimates the other side. Like in World War I, the soldiers of both sides cheerfully went to war, thinking it would soon be over and they will go home by Christmas. Each side saw to it that the other side does not win. So the conflict grew, with the hope that additional troops and/or powers would finish the job. By now it was a truly world war.

Meanwhile, the protagonist studying conflict, was so absorbed in the study, he neglected his wife and family. To get his attention, the wife pretended to have a boyfriend. In retaliation, the husband/protagonist got a lady friend to keep him company while he was writing his story. The personal conflict kept escalating into a mini-war, ending in courts. Hence, the protagonist and his wife personified how large conflicts grow from small differences, which if not squelched quickly, would likely grow into large one, on the personal scale. On the international scale, the small differences, if not resolved quickly, would mushroom into a world war.

The author can provide his/her own protagonist, with a different set of differences and/or grievances, which may include murder, as the ultimate irreparable damage, resulting from unresolved conflict.

Raising Clones

The biologist who cloned his parents, before they died, is faced with baby parents, whom he raises, as close as they were raised, so he would be as close to his adult parents as possible when the clones grow up. He sends the child cloned parents to schools that are same type as his departed parents had attended. In addition, he would teach the clones any "Old Country" proverbs and other quirks, which would make the nostalgic scientist feel the illusion that his dearly departed parents are back with him at home. He might have to borrow from the techniques of Dr. Dolittle. At some point in the adult future of the parent clones, the biologist may be tempted to call them Mom and Dad, with carefully planned reactions from the parent clones.

The writer could work out a plot for visiting guests who knew the parents of the scientist. How he would explain the matter, at home and later when going out with the cloned parents.

Stolen Ashes

The house of a guy, call him Sam, is burglarized, and a precious antique pottery from a Chinese dynasty, was stolen. What made the crime even worse, the container held the ashes of the Sam's dear mother. He was now determined to find his mom's ashes, and restore into a holder worthy of all the memories he had of her. First, Sam worked with the Police, who had more pressing things to do than find some ashes. So Sam puts an ad in the paper, offering a ten thousand dollar reward for anyone who returns his mother's ashes—no questions asked. Someone calls to Sam he was returning those ashes. That he expected to be paid, as promised. But the ash holder looked different, and Sam could not be sure these were his mother's ashes.

The writer can build on this premise and create a plot that would take the reader on an exciting roller coaster ride to the end.

"DEAD" MAN'S PENSION

A bisexual guy, name him Paul, is tired of working hard, and wishes to retire early—in fact too early for eligibility. He fakes his death. Later he dresses up as a woman and collects the pension as Paul's widow.

The writer could pursue the story in one of many directions:

a) Paul gets away with it for a while, until someone recognizes him in a gay bar. The author will concoct interesting ways of handling this situation;
b) A former colleague of Paul, meets the "widow", say Ingrid, falls in love with her and wants to marry "her" not knowing the real story behind the caper.
c) Irma meets a gay former co-worker, who has figured out the plan, and wants to do the same, and use their combined "widow" incomes to have a nice house and live comfortably "ever after". The writer may inject some intrigue and outside spying into the plot—perhaps including blackmail and/or attempts at extortion.
d) The author can come up with his/her own plot and set of characters from her/his own experiences in life. There are many possibilities of resolving the final episode in this mystery.

Reward on Terrorist

A terrorist, Ahmed, is wanted by the US, offering a 5 million dollar reward for information that leads to his capture. He belongs to a highly secret organization, which is headed by Hassan, and is unknown to the US. Ahmed falls out with his boss, Hassan, who sends an obscure member, Ali, to inform the US on Ahmed, and then collect the 5 million dollar reward for the highly secretive terrorist clique. It desperately needs such funds to conduct their operations against the US and its allies. To the US, the informer presents himself as a law abiding citizen, who seeks peace and stability for his troubled country.

The author has several options to follow with his/her story line:

a) Ali gets the 5 million reward from the US, and passes the whole amount to the organization, which elevates him to deputy boss, or some such rank; OR
b) Ali gets the 5 million dollars, BUT keeps half of it, then passes only half of it to the organization, one OR
c) The US is aware of the plot, but pretends it does not know, so as to find out all important members of the organization, then possibly nab them, before they conduct fatal operations. The author can create a plot that facilitates this aim of the US, perhaps pockmarked with unexpected pitfalls and setbacks, before the final denouement; OR
d) Ahmed gets wind of the reward windfall, and wants in on the reward, or he would foil the conspiracy, and no one ends up with a penny from the 5 million reward; OR
e) After irreconcilable differences with his former boss, Ahmed ends up working with the CIA, who grabs all the important members of the terrorist clique, before they do any damage. Meanwhile any reward for Ahmed could be the subject of another subplot by the writer.

Leonardo da Vinci Revisits his Art

Time machine operator brings Leonardo da Vinci back over here. He is taken to the Louvre, and comments on the Mona Lisa, with terse and uncomplimentary remarks about his former model. He reveals secrets we did not know. Dressed and over-bearded for our times, da Vinci is dragged to a Sotheby auction, where he watches one of his sketches go for 5 million dollars. When his guide explains how much that money is in Italy of the fifteenth/sixteenth century, Leonardo almost faints: to think that he lived so frugally, when his art would be so valuable. The writer can inject creative comments, with old local Italian flavor, starting with Florence, then Rome and ending in Venice. Said author may find or create character quirks for da Vinci, and insert them into the story. The contrast between the atmosphere and life in fifteen and sixteenth century Italy, and of that in current Europe and the New World, can be exciting--rotating around a good story line.

Reaction of da Vinci to the hordes of tourists mesmerized by the Mona Lisa, and the "insane" amounts of money paid for Leonardo's "doodles" can be fascinating, with an inventive writer. Also, reaction of the public watching a Leonardo "impersonator" watching the works of da Vinci can be intriguing, with the pen of a good writer. For lunch, the author can take Leonardo to an Italian restaurant, featuring Pizza. Leonardo may be intrigued by the name, and may recall things about the city and Tower of Pizza. He may have comments about pasta, and why it was in the Last Supper.

No Gravity

A new phenomenon hit our planet. For one day in July, Earth lost its gravity. Cars and trains were floating in the air. At home, the chairs and tables were off the ground and so were the people, who sat in these eerie floating chairs. Pets and their food pots were up there, and it was quite an effort to bring them together so the poor creatures can eat and drink to survive. Their barking and meowing was quite a sight.

Airplanes, in the air did not know how to land. When stable in the air, near the ground, the passengers would jump off the plane, but would stay floating, with no gravity to pull them to the ground. These flying aircraft stayed close to ground, so that when gravity returned, they would not drop to earth and cause damage and casualties.

The write can use his/her imagination as how to handle the ships in the ocean, and what happens to the seas, when gravity is temporarily gone.

This unique event is investigated by scientists and all branches of the government. The theories range from black holes, to highly advanced aliens, trying to disrupt resistance on Earth, so they can take over the planet, with little effort, considering their small force, invading from outer space.

After about a day, gravity can return in one of two ways:

a) Gravity returns gradually, giving earthlings time to adjust, and prevent airplanes and flying objects from crashing to the ground; OR
b) The restoration of gravity is sudden, causing flying aircrafts to crash to the ground, with horrendous cumulative damage and casualties. Any cars or other objects would just drop to the ground, from whatever heights they would be floating at.

To avoid disasters in a future similar event, laws are passed wherein, any car or object not in motion, would be tied to the ground with an anchoring rope. Doghouses and pet cages must be secured to the floor.

The Government commissions the best scientific brains to study this temporary loss of gravity, to see if it is something science had ignored, or something more sinister is happening, like interference from Extra Terrestrial Aliens (ETA's). Here, the author could follow either path. But the more credible path would be highly advance ETA's with few in numbers, but armed with out-of-this-world technological capabilities, to compensate for their sparse numbers, that aims to take over the planet. Further analysis of ETA's home planet may indicate a catastrophic event had happened there, requiring the inhabitants to look for another planet to survive. Their calamity could be a natural happening, with the inhabitants having had no hand in it; OR, the destruction could be the result of conflicts amongst the inhabitants of the planet themselves. The author can follow a number of plot options to follow this part of the story line for the reader.

Enslaved Planet

Planet Earth is subdued and the humans are enslaved by a technologically far superior ETA's who had abandoned their destroyed planet. They used no-gravity techniques to disrupt life on Earth, in the process of securing the planet for themselves. Once they did that, each human was tattooed with a barcode, which would be recorded in very sophisticated super computer. Having registered all humans, of all ages, thusly, the administrative ETA's then did a similar registration on all the animals they could get hold of. They seem to crave protein, which their home planet must have exhausted, in their calamity.

The author can pursue many possibilities. In one story line, as the ETA's eat more meat and protein, they seem to reproduce more and multiply in shorter time than before. Soon they populate the whole planet, while they continue to reproduce prolifically.

Strange types of dwellings sprout everywhere. Here the writer can use his imagination to come up with type of homes, and why it suits this type of creatures, because they look so-and-so and they behave in such-and-such manner.

To accommodate ETA's voracious appetite for meat, food markets pop up everywhere, with all kinds of meat on display. They include cuts of all sizes from cows, horses and rodents to humans. Some meats are packaged and frozen, others are fresh.

Here, the author may dramatize the human meat on display, by having some humans—characters, who are still alive, pass by the market. One of them recognizes the fresh meat on display, and gets sick. A

The writer may take the opportunity to philosophize, as to how humans had treated the animals just for their meat, ignoring their feelings and their social ways and emotions amongst themselves. Now that they see humans being similarly treated by ETA's, the survivors of our species may treat other animals differently, if they ever get out of this crisis.

Guy with the Glowing Dick

Richard was born with a penis that glows in the dark. His mom took him to all kinds of specialists. The consensus was that it was the result of a freak genetic mutation, similar to some of the sea creatures that glow in dark sea waters. Other mutations render certain fish transparent.

The writer now has a grown male character, who has a male organ that glows in the dark. The author has a choice of several story lines:

1) Richard can be the subject of medical studies. During that, he falls in love with one of his examiners. The writer has the option of having his lover as a female, or male. The plot could get more intriguing when Richard's lover/examiner notices that as Richard gets more emotional, the glow of his organ intensifies. This complicates the relationship, and threatens to transform a love affair into a freak show;
2) Another story line would involve a clever circus operator, or a country fair manager manipulating Richard into a freak show for a lucrative reward. The writer will select his type of conniving character, who will play some sneaky plans, or tricks to persuade Richard to join the show he is staging. There will be twists and turns, and perhaps some heartache.
3) Richard's experience when he takes his date to bed. How he goes about it and his partner takes this intimate act with a guy whose organ glows. The writer can devise a believable plot, and realistic dialogue, through this event. Some humor may be injected in a power failure, with total darkness, except for Richard's glowing penis that throws some guiding light into a pitch dark room.

Gay Potion

A creative person develops a potion that renders its drinker temporarily gay. The author can develop the plot in different ways:

1) A Jamaican voodoo man mixes up a brew to chase out the evil spirits from his straight nephew. To his surprise, the nephew turns gay soon after drinking the potion—if only temporarily. This unusual potion comes to the attention of US tourist, Jerry, a businessman who is visiting Jamaica. The voodoo man thought he had a useless brew, and was about to dump it. Just before that, Jerry buys it for a few dollars, and flies back to the US with a whole jug-full of this gay potion.
   The author can come up with some interesting story lines, with Jerry's gay potion and what he does with it in the mainland. If the writer makes Jerry a gay character, does he give the potion to unsuspecting straight men, and then seduce them. If the "victims" find out, which way does the plot go? Into litigation or vengeful murder?
2) An American chemist, Morgan, accidentally develops a drug that temporarily renders a straight man gay. Morgan does not immediately know what he has discovered, thinking it acted like an aspirin. A guest tries it, after a headache, and soon tries to make out with Morgan. The writer can develop the story line with that theme in mind;
3) Jerry finds out that the same potion renders a gay person temporarily straight. When the evangelical community gets wind of this magic brew, Jerry becomes the toast of town. The chief exorcist offers a lot of money for the whole jug of gay-reform potion. The author can develop this plot in many different fascinating directions;
4) Chemist Morgan's drug has a similar effect on gay persons, who turn temporarily straight. He gets FDA approval as a headache remedy. But the rumor gets out to a strict religious sect, that Morgan's drug "cures homosexuality". They immediately buy a

large supply and use on the religious gays who have come there to reform and find God again. The writer can pursue this and find out how successful the "gay cleansers" will be. The legal profession, the gay community as well as certain elected government officials can weigh in, on this moral matter.

Leaders in Love

Two world leaders meet privately, like at Camp David, to solve a touchy world problem amongst themselves, with no aids present, to avoid any leaks in private conversations. Somehow, the 2 leaders more than "hit it off". They fall in love.

This main theme may be pursued in a number of directions:

1) The 2 heads of state are both male bisexuals. In their first encounter they have sex, and now there is no going back to normal. But for the public, they act like before, as they carry on a private affair. The writer can develop the plot in many ways, and decides when the rumors start, and what they do about it. The cartoonists could have a field day, while the spouses get into arguments at home, perhaps spilling over into the public arena by filing for divorce;
2) One head of state is male, while the other is female. The author may pursue a story line of great secrecy and public manipulations, to continue this very sensitive, but, to them, overwhelming affair. One means of communications would be secure e-mails. If and when the e-mail server is hacked, that's when the affair hits the fan. One meeting place could be one of them visits a remote resort in the lover's country—ostensibly for vacation. While the visiting leader is there, the host head of state sneaks into this faraway resort. The author can inject a scandal in the affair when and where he/she chooses.

The Pyramids Disappear

Extraterrestrials with advanced technology, secretly materialize at Egypt's Great Pyramid, at Giza. They use their matter transfer knowhow to transmit the pyramids to their planet, then similarly transmit themselves back to their home planet.

Intriguing story lines can evolve from the basic premise. It could start with an embarrassing press release by the Egyptian Government, that "the Great Pyramid has disappeared". It could coincide with the date of April 1. Of course everyone would believe that is a April Fool's Day story—"a very funny one at that", will comment the TV's talking heads.

From there, the plot can develop in different directions:

1) As the true facts emerge, the United Nations committee on historic sites meets in emergency session, to recommend a course of action. The discussion could appear humorous to the public, as they talk about the inexplicable disappearance of a huge pyramid in one dark night. The science consultants then explain how the pyramid was stolen. Then they speculate as to what planet the pyramid could have gone, and if Earth folks could possibly get there. Even if our astronauts get to that planet, they could not transmit the pyramid back to Earth, with their inferior technology.
2) The world could resign to the loss of the Great Pyramid, but now concentrates on protecting all the other historic sites. But how? That would be the theme of the highly technical discussions. How to detect the arrival of these Extraterrestrials. Then what? What to do when they are at the next World Heritage spot?

The creative sci fi aptitude of the writer will kick in here, to take the story into uncharted territory, perhaps. Would the Big Powers of Planet Earth cooperate on a mission to the culprit planet? Not just to retrieve a pyramid, but perhaps to also learn their super advanced technical skills.

Divine Competition

Christians' God and Muslim's Allah are locked into apocalyptic competition. The believers of each side have been claiming that their Leader is superior to the other. For centuries, God's angels have been compiling a data base of prayer requests from His Christians. Simultaneously, Allah's malaika (angel equivalent) were busy on the Muslims ledger, with columns of good deed credits and ill will debits, in preparation for the Day of Rising (from the graves). Constant prayers to Allah requested that He show God of the Christians that He is just as powerful, despite their disparaging prayers.

God sends Jesus to Hawaii during the water skiing contests. He slides on the ocean waves without skis, and beats the best of them, zooming on first rate skis. Allah counters by creating a camel that can walk in the desert for two months without food and drink. A panel of holy men from both sides agree that both miracles are equivalent, and cancel each other out. So we are back where we started.

The writer can expand on this theme into a conclusion, as to whose Big Chief is more powerful.

Rome's "Jerry Springer"

Citizens of Rome get tired of gladiators fighting and lions mauling Christians. During a lull in the Coliseum, a fighting couple were chasing each other, and accidentally entered the Coliseum, while arguing and punching each other. The crowds who came to see others fight, cheered the new violent competitors, with some cheering the man, while the others cheered the woman. This started a new tradition in the Coliseum, with a Jerry Springer type of disputes settled there. The Roman "Jerry Springer" would get a good monetary reward for finding the dysfunctional couples and arranging their dispute settlement in the Coliseum for a share of the monetary reward for the sparring couples and any side lovers in the dispute. If the couple do not settle, then they are given a choice of weapons, to battle with till one of them violently prevails.

The writer can use creativity to devise a plot based on this premise, and pursue it to the end, contrasting today's Jerry Springer type of disputes and settlements, with Roman times with no holds barred, and a coliseum audience itching for blood sports.

Dwarf Heir to Throne

The king of a realm has one offspring to inherit the throne, and he is a dwarf.

The writer can build on this premise in any of a host of directions:

1) The Royal Dwarf could be very intelligent, and the King may insist on grooming him to rule the kingdom and demand respect for him from his subjects;
2) The King may pick one of his tall subjects, with facial features very similar to his short son, to stand in for him in public, as the heir. After the king dies, the stand-in, may try to take over as the new king, while putting away the legitimate dwarf king. Since very few of the subjects had seen the short heir before his father died, the stand-in, fake king may get away with it for a while. The story line could get into twists and turns, especially if the Royal Dwarf escapes and tries to organize loyalists to reclaim his legitimate throne. The heir's small size heading a fighting force may not appeal to some of his subjects. The writer can wade through that with a creative plot.

Interactive God

Traveling astronauts come across a planet, call it G, where the inhabitants deal with an interactive God. He responds to their prayers directly by a voice from the clouds or bushes. Sometimes He responds through the telephone, sends clouds in the sky, arranged in a form with a written message. Despite all that no one has seen their God in person.

The author can use this concept to arrange a plot that contrasts with the mysterious unverified God of planet Earth. On planet G no one asks: "Do you believe in God," since He is there dealing with them every day.

Motel E. T.

Extra Terrestrials run a motel in the Mojave Desert area. Their appearance is especially fixed to look like normal Earth's inhabitants. They have been thoroughly trained to act like Earth people. In the motel, the ET's provide the room rentals, but also evaluate each guest, as to whether he/she could be trained in ET' planet. If yes, the guest, along with other qualified persons, are tranquilized and put in a secretly housed spaceship, which takes the involuntary recruits to the ET planet. While there, the Earth people are thoroughly transformed mentally and emotionally to obey the ET, while keeping their normal Earth appearance. After that, the trained recruits are sent back to Earth to help carry out the ET's grand plan to take over this planet for ET's use, to supply food and minerals to a starved ET planet.

The author can pick a story line that leads to Earth people suspecting something sinister. The plot could call on the psychological community to evaluate the behavior of the "assimilated" ET's and the trained Earth subjects. The writer can pursue the plot accordingly, leading to perhaps a conflict with ET. The type of conflict could be devised, with a creative ending.

People's Court

We are in a mythical country, where all the lawyers and judges have left for lucrative jobs in other countries. As a last resort, the authorities allow the aggrieved to haul the accused into makeshift People's Court. Here, both sides agree on a jury, then present their cases, without the benefit of a lawyer, or a judge's supervision.

The writer has many avenues for an interesting plot. He/she can pick from a plethora of different characters for the aggrieved and the accused. Same goes for the jury. Since lawyers and judges are not involved, the case would hinge on the way facts are presented, a lot of emotion and perhaps good "Hollywood" acting, with no reference to any legal precedence.

Some cases could be circus like, others could be well done. Still a few could end up in violence, with the bailiff not sure who to obey.

Super Others

We know that Superman does great physical feats. In our modern life we really need:

1. Super-Banker takes off to save the desperate homeowner from eviction and imminent homelessness. Wearing his Super-Banker cape, which billows as he swoops onto the widow's house, where the Sheriff is forcing the old woman out of her lifetime home, to complete the foreclosure. Super-banker lands on the front entrance of the house, with payoff check in hand and gives it to the Sheriff, as he escorts the widow back into her abode. The Sheriff walks away with the check, as the old woman moves back into her home. And Super-Banker takes off to save the next victim, as the widow's neighbors cheer him on.
2. Super-Doctor flies off, with hospital uniform flapping in the air. He heads for the home of a terminal man, and lands next to his bedside, where sniffing relatives cannot conceal their sorrow. He sprays a magic medical powder on the dying patient, who suddenly straightens up, rises and gets out of bed, to the incredulity of everyone there. The patient tells his tearful relatives, that he feels fine; for them to stop crying; it depresses him.

Super-Doctor then takes off as the cheering hospital visitors waved vigorously at him.

The writer may pick any other Super-Professional and build a similar story around him/her. It could be Super-Teacher, Super-Nurse, Super-Mechanic. There could be a limit: for instance, what could a Super-Politician do?

Anyway, it is emulating the super deeds of Superman, but in a much more needed way in modern day.

WINNING LOTTERY TICKET

A poor hungry passerby sees a lottery ticket on the dashboard of a car. He opens the unlocked car door and walks off with the ticket, figuring even a $2 win can buy him a few chicken nuggets at Macdonald's. The ticket wins $15 million dollar.

The author can start with this premise, and take the story a number of different directions:

1. The legal owner of the winning ticket does not know he/she had won anything. The ticket thief gets the millions. His conscience bothers him about the legitimate ticket buyer. He finds his address. The ticket thief can then compensate the victim in a number of ways, without telling him how he got his money, and save a legal forfeiture. The author has options here.
2. The legal ticket owner knows his lottery numbers, and finds out he/she is the winner, before returning to his parked car. When he does not find the ticket in the car, he rushes home to find it.

The writer can pursue the story from this angle.

SUPER GAY

Gay superman roams the world, in his billowing rainbow colored cape, to rescue gay men from persecution, torture and even death, as a result of prejudice in a homophobic society. A man is being brutally beaten up in Uganda. Super Gay gets wind of, and takes off for that country, and swoops down on the heartless men doing the beating. He plucks them off the victim, one by one, and flings them a hundred feet away in different directions. Super Gay then lifts the gay victim and carries him to a loving gay home, where he is patched up and given a loving home.

The writer can think up specific cases for Super Gay to solve, using his/her own characters, taken from their own life's experiences. The cases could parallel famous ones over the years, such as Mathew, whose body was left on fence, in a Midwestern farm. Many other cases wherein their own homophobic parents kick their gay kid out in the cold, as soon as they find out he is gay.

The writer can also adopt a powerful justice seeker, Super Lesbo, who is a super woman, that rescues lesbians from inhuman treatment any place on Earth, where persecution and killing of lesbians is condoned. The author can create his own type of Super Lesbo, and use realistic victims similar to the ones in real life, who go through hell in a prejudiced society. The press archives is full of cases of prejudice and persecution of lesbians. The writer's victim characters could be similar to actual ones in those archives, to give the fictional story a realistic premise. Or the author may very well have personal knowledge or experience about real life characters, whether being a cruel persecutor, or one of the victims in the story.

Mafia's Fancy Dress Summit

Some years ago, a Mafia summit in an obscure New York State location caught the attention of the FBI, whose operatives swooped in and arrested all the big Mafia figures of the time. Ever since then, the mob bosses have avoided top level meetings.

BUT the idea of this plot will ostensibly ensure a successful high level meeting for the Mafia chiefs, without Government interference. Even if the FBI people sneak into the event, they will not know who is in attendance, and whether they are innocent civilians or Mafia bosses.

The author will create a fancy dress event, open to known friends and relatives, as well as the mob chiefs. They will arrive in their cars already in various types of fancy dress. Each one will fold a sleeve with their initials on. If a boss is unknown to another boss, he will very discreetly unfold the sleeve, in a shadowy corner, and find out the name of mob chief he would be dealing with.

The plot can provide many possibilities, such as the FBI trying to find who is attending the meeting, which room, and how to find the names of the mob bosses. Would they find out about the names on the folded sleeves? The writer can create a story line along these lines, or move it into other paths, based on the "fancy dress" premise of a top level conference amongst the Mafia chiefs.

Planet of Dead Movie Stars

Astronauts come across a strange, but habitable new planet. They land and explore for minerals or signs of life. To their shock and surprise, they find famous human beings, who used to live on planet Earth. They recognized Boris Karloff, Peter Lorre, and many others. After their death, they woke up on this new planet. The former Earth actors, were busy doing the same thing on this newly discovered planet. One of the astronauts is an evangelical, and tries to figure out if the resurrected dead here, are supposed to be in Heaven or Hell. He evaluated the sins of each movie star, to see if they deserved Hell, or whether they were minor enough, to be ignored, qualifying for admission to Heaven.

The writer could pursue this basic premise and incorporate it into his own custom made story line, with his/her chosen characters. The tale need not be confined to movie stars. It could encompass ordinary people after Armageddon. The astronauts could recognize some of their old dead folks over at this planet. Such speculation will be whether Hell or Heaven is located on some planet; whether both places are on different areas of the same planet, or whether Heaven is in a separate planet. That would make Hell's location on another separate planet. If Hell and Heaven is on the same planet, must not rotate around itself, but just orbits its sun. Thus, one side of the planet permanently faces the scorching sun, causing permanent Hell's fires, while the other side does not get the sun, is engulfed in lush vegetation.

The author can pursue a plot based on this basic premise, with chosen characters following a creative story line. He/she could a famous actor who went to Hell, and another who went to Heaven. Their stories could be separate, or interconnected.

Pen Bomb

A man planning an assassination develops a miniature, but powerful pipe bomb disguised as a pen. He aims to kill the chairman at a conference table, where a meeting is scheduled. He places the pen/bomb at the head of the table, where the chairman would be sitting and taking notes. The would-be killer then disappears outside the building.

Later the meeting convenes, discussions start and the chairman reaches for the pen to take notes. He presses the pen against the note book to write. A strong enough explosion kills the targeted chairman.

The writer can lay out his/her plot from this basic premise, which could be varied as to location, type of event and what kind of target. The author could go into different directions from here. The plot could be international after a nuclear scientist, or it could be a jealous colleague who has been overlooked over an important promotion.

Adopted Robot

Futuristic society where the high population has lead to severely limiting the number of children being born. Families resort to adopting advance robots, whose software allows them to continuously learn and grow up mentally and emotionally with the years, as each Rob (for Robot) advances in the years with its adopted family. After a while Rob feels and acts like a human being and a member of the family.

The writer could use this premise to develop a story line in a choice of many directions:

1. Can Rob be kind and emotional like human beings? Of course "It" will have much better memory than its human family. Is it capable of crime, growing up, say in a mob-type of family?
2. Would adopted Robots from other families get together to take over their city and save it from the "dysfunctional" humans?

These and other possibilities may be explored by the author.

Russian Laser

Russia develops a powerful devastating laser that could obliterate anything from a long distance. Placed on the moon, it can obliterate any location it remotely aims from the Earth. When ready, Russia then demands from the West to return all those lands and countries they "stole" from Russia. Otherwise, the Giant Laser will start leveling one city after another, until Russian demands are met, starting with the Baltic States, to be removed from NATO control and returned to Russian hegemony.

The author may base a story line on this basic assumption and develop a plot to accommodate this, and incorporate it in the current state of international affairs going into a dive. Lots of options are available for selecting protagonists, as well as villains and heroes.

ARRANGED ACCIDENT

A wealthy man has a jet plane, and flies out of a local private airport. His son, call him Walter is the sole heir, and learns that his dad is about to change his will, and leave his fortune to charities. The dad has an appointment with his attorney in two days. Walter has this short time to prevent the change in the will, which currently leaves all of the Old Man's possessions and money to him, his only son. Walter lures an airport mechanic he associates with, to tamper with his dad's airplane's fuel gage, to read "Full", after the mechanic empties the tank. The reward for the mechanic: a percentage of Walter's inheritance.

The writer may vary the basic theme of this story idea. The inheritance could go to Walter's rival sibling. OR the new will could grant the inheritance to the father's favorite pet, setting the stage for a post mortem court fight, wherein Walter would question his father's mental competence when the will was drafted. Walter could investigate the attorney, as to why he went along with the new will, "knowing" that his dad was mentally incompetent. The author could precede with a denouement of the plot, with protagonists that suits him.

X-Ray Eyed Inhabitants

Astronauts stumble on a planet with different type of inhabitants, compared with the Earth's human beings. In addition to that, the creatures of that planet have x-ray eyes. This is why they are all naked in fair weather. The reason is easy to fathom; no matter what kind of clothes they wear, their x-ray eyes see past that to the walking skeleton. With the special eye glasses, which many of them wear, they can see the naked bodies of others, even if they cover their bodies, when the weather is cold.

A plot based on this premise would include how the astronauts deal with beings of this sort. The writer could decide as to the level of intelligence of these creatures. What if they took back a couple with them to Earth, to reproduce their species, there. Those x-ray eyes could come in handy for security surveillance at airports and Federal buildings. First the author has to figure out their biology. Can they survive on planet Earth, as is. If not, what do researches recommend, to enable the creatures to survive on Earth. There could be other plot variations, depending on how to adjust events, based on the basic premise of the story idea.

Pregnant Man Wins the Reward

Marcus, a billionaire seeker of publicity announces a $1 million reward for the first man who gets pregnant. Everyone dismisses it as an impossible prank, except one guy in San Francisco, living with his burly and muscular macho lover, Caesar. The couple goes to Marcus, to collect their reward. At the gated estate, they are met with fences and guard dogs on the other side. Caesar tries to pull the fences down to get to Marcus and collect the million dollars. The guards call the policed and arrest the couple. In jail, a pro-bono lawyer, Howard Dingle, needing self promotion, takes on the case. Lo and behold, the lawyer can verify that Caesar's lover is actually pregnant, and will give birth in 3 months. In court, the evidence and witnesses testify for both sides. Marcus' legal team try to prove it is all a fraud. But Dingle counters their arguments with solid evidence.

The theme can be tweaked to fit the writer's own characters, and desired story line and ending.

Poisonous Fruit

A man, George, with a deep grudge against a former work colleague, Harry, seeks revenge, for unjustly causing George to get fired from his job, which cost his family's precious livelihood. George lives in a nice neighborhood, with a spacious yard and fruit trees of orange, apple and others. There are also planted tomatoes, eggplant and various vegetables. When George and family are on vacation, Harry sneaks in under cover of darkness, carrying an injection syringe with poisonous liquid inside. He injects the deadly poison into several oranges and tomatoes, and then quietly departs without anyone noticing.

The writer can use his/her imagination as to what happens when George and family return; like who eats what, when and what happens. How the investigations start, and forensic techniques used to find the killer. What the curious neighbors gossip and do—pointing fingers at innocent parties, maybe. The author will have his/her own cast of characters, who will do the "show" to an interesting end, hopefully.

Tampered Fruit

A variation of "Poisonous Fruit", above, would be for a family prankster, or jokester, to inject marijuana or strong alcoholic drinks into the fruits, using a syringe, or similar technique. The writer would pick one such idea, and build a mystery drama, or a humorous story line around the basic idea.

Spring Baseball

An outfielder, nicknamed 'Jumpy', who is on a certain baseball team, Oakland A's, let's say, is famous for catching most any fly ball that comes in his direction, because he can jump higher than anybody, who ever played the game. For that he won the Gold Glove and other awards. After the game, Jumpy packs and keeps his own shoes, while the Equipment Manager takes care of all other stuff for Jumpy and all the other players, who also leave their shoes for the Manager to take custody, till the next game. One day after the game, Jumpy walks to his car, carrying tote bag of belongings, including his valued game shoes. A teenager and baseball fan, riding a skateboard, hits Jumpy, knocking him down, while his tote bag is flung several feet. It falls on hard ground and scatters the contents, including Jumpy's shoes, which are seriously damaged, exposing wires and batteries out of the shoes. The teen picks up one shoe, as a souvenir, and dashes away with it, before he is forced to give it back to Jumpy, even though the shoe is obviously badly damaged, with wires sticking out and a battery dangling from the side.

At home, the teen skateboarder, call him Speedy, examines his idol's shoe, and finds out it is especially made with powerful metal spring that compresses into the heel of the shoe, with slick flat battery that snugly fits in a sheath, on the side of the shoe. A button near the toe, when pressed, releases the spring. That is when Jumpy leaps in the air to catch a fly ball. Speedy was disappointed and terribly disillusioned that his favorite player was cheating when doing his sensational catches.

The author takes it from here to develop the story line. What does Speedy do next? Does he blackmail Jumpy? Would he go to the Baseball Commissioner? Would Jumpy catch up with Speedy before his reputation is ruined? Does Jumpy take the potential scandal seriously enough to contemplate hiring a hit man? The writer will have a host of choices for the direction of taking this topical and seasonal story to and interesting and perhaps a unique ending.

Life, the Conveyor Belt

A certain person, call him 'Jimmy', is born at the start of his Conveyor Belt, which carries him from baby, to teenager, to adult, to retired old man, and finally deposits Jimmy at his grave. As the Belt passes by the years, Jimmy grows up, graduates, marries, raises a family, retires, then dies when the Conveyor Belt reaches his final resting place. The philosophical point is that despite growing up and all the achievements, Jimmy is on a journey that will end in the cemetery. The daily spin about life, being happy, successful, etc. will not change the fact that it will all end in the cemetery, or the urn of cremated ashes. Being optimistic or pessimistic about life will not alter that basic fact that the Belt conveys us from conception to internment.

The Writer can base a plot and a cast of characters that readers can identify with, into an absorbing story from cradle to grave. It is not meant to depress people but to show dispassionate facts of life.

The Great US Wall

The US builds a Great Wall along the Mexican American border. It will be a replica of the Great Wall of China. There are 2 purposes for it:

1. A good tourist attraction, just like the Chinese Wall. In addition, the wide pathway on top would be used for races and tournaments, past the turrets and observation posts;
2. Keep illegal immigrants out of the US.

Two forces would be working at the Great US Wall:

a) At the top, would be organized competition and advertized entertainment, with many professionals busy creating fun for everyone;
b) Under the Wall, there are tunnels being built by drug traffickers to smuggle heroin, cocaine, etc. into the US, from Mexico.

The story line will tell two parallel stories tied to the same border wall. Above the Wall, will be the tough stance of guards and drones, all along the Great Border Wall. Underneath the same wall will be the secret army of drug cartels burrowing tunnels to import their deadly products into the US. The author can use this theme to plot a story line highlighting the tug of war between these two formidable forces, and plan an absorbing denouement, telling us who wins the conflict.

Interview with Jesus

Someone discovers a scroll in an obscure overlooked cave on the West Bank of Palestine. When carefully unrolled and examined, it is found to be an interview of Jesus by a representative of Pontius Pilot.

The writer will create a story line highlighting this interview. He/she will carefully prepare the key questions that were supposedly asked. The replies of Jesus will, perhaps, include some of His famous parables. The interview session would be grave. The direction of Roman questioning would be to justify the crucifixion, to please the local Jewish leaders. Much of the plot would be realistic imagination, because no record of such an interview exists, even though it must have taken place at the time.

Horse of Alexander the Great: Autobiography

Pick a favorite horse of Alexander the Great, and create an autobiography, with the great horse telling us the details of battles, from its point of view. If the name of the horse is not known, perhaps the author can invent a realistic name for the times, like Olympus. The horse will describe Alexander from its point of view; how he rode and treated Olympus, in war and peace. The writer could pick a specific famous battle, and have the horse describe it from its vantage position, and whether Olympus or his master got hurt or wounded, how and where in the battle.

The story could also make for an animated movie.

Attempt at the Queen

During the State Opening of Parliament, the British Monarch is in the Royal Carriage being drawn by a team of horses. A conspiracy is hatched by enemies of the state, wherein a giant firecracker is hurled in front of the lead horses of the carriage. The pulling horses get spooked, and take off with the carriage, way out in the country, where the conspirators catch up and kidnap the Monarch.

The author may adopt this theme to develop a story line, as to what happens next. Will there be a Royal Ransom? How much? Where will it be delivered? To buy time, the authorities play along to buy time, till Scotland Yard gathers all the identifying information, for a decisive action. Relevant information must be compiled first. Where is the Monarch kept? When is it safe to attack, without endangering any life? Whether it succeeds first time, is up to the writer and his/her detailed outline of the story plot. The writer will have options as to final denouement.

Parallel Planet

Astronauts land on a living planet, which is inhabited by creatures much like humans on Earth. But they noticed distinct differences in behavior. For instance, the house of worship the astronauts came across, had a gun at the steeple, and another gun fixed to the entrance door. Since the atmosphere was similar to Earth, they took off their space helmets and suits, and slipped into this building, where people were congregating peacefully it seems. There are pews like in churches on Earth. The high priest arrives. He wears a black overall robe. He initiates the service, by taking a pistol out of a pocket, points it to his forehead, and pulls the trigger, and a loud bang is heard; but the priest does not fall dead. Nor is he hurt. Apparently, it is a harmless ritual. Looking into their holy book, there is a painting of their prophet being shot by some military person of a foreign power, it appears. So the gun has become the symbol of their faith, since the execution of their prophet, when they were occupied by the foreign forces, many years before.

The author can use this theme to compare with the rituals that developed on Earth, such as recalling the crucifixion every time someone makes the signs of the cross. If the writer chooses a different way the planet's prophet was killed, he/she can change the prayer initiation, to reflect the type of death chosen for the planet's prophet. This could also be a dispassionate look at how rituals develop and followed without much thought.

One Strike per Name

A criminal, call him Alan, has 3 assumed names. He has been jailed separately under each assumed name. The authorities do not know that this same person has committed a total of 3 felonies, qualifying for the 3-strike-you're-out sentence. Jerry, an acquaintance of Alan, learns about the 3 felonies, and decides to blackmail him for money, since Jerry has run into financial trouble. Alan has served his last individual felony sentence, using one of the 3 false names, and is now free. But Jerry can get him locked up for life, under the 3-felony law, perpetrated by one person.

The writer can adopt this theme for an interesting story line, to tell readers which way it is going. Will there be murder? Will there be payoff? Perhaps some other direction the author can take us. Will others be involved? Who can they be--Friends, relatives, fellow criminals? It could be made into a page turner for the reader.

Dead Twice?

Disgruntled employee, call him 'Sam', intent on revenge from his cruel boss, Thad say, sneaks into his bachelor home, and shoots him, not knowing that his boss was already dead from a heart attack. Sam gets arrested and tried for murder.

The writer could base a plot on this premise. Options include:

1. A brilliant lawyer and a lot of accurate forensic scientific work prove that Sam merely shot a dead corpse;
2. Sam is found guilty and sentenced, and serves a number of years, before the Innocents Project examines the case, and finds him innocent of murder;
3. A former girlfriend of Thad comes forward and states that Thad had the heart attack while having sex with her. That she was too ashamed to come forward before.

The writer may use any or a combination of these options to advance the plot of this mystery story to a logical conclusion.

Coping with Government Laws

A comic story, in which an activist forms a movement, Clear Language, which demands that the government pay for the mental health of citizens, who cannot cope with all the government laws and regulations, and mentally breakdown.

The author can carry this theme into many different directions:

1. The authorities charge him with disturbing the peace, but is released upon court order, only to resume his crusade for free mental care from complicated government laws and regulations;
2. The movement gains popularity and forces the government to simplify procedures so that a twelve year old can understand them. So every time a regulation is written, the members of Clear Language meet. They bring into the session a 12-year boy or girl, read the regulation to him/her, in a clear loud voice, on the speaker's stand. The president of Clear Language then asks the boy or girl: "Did you completely understand this law (or regulation)?" If he/she answers "yes", then Clear Language votes for approval. If the reply is negative, then group organize a series of protests, to force the government to rescind the law/regulation, or to simplify it so that their smart 12-year old witness can understand what the hell the government is talking about!
3. The writer may have a completely different alternative, which suits his own characters and experience.

Tax by IQ

In a futuristic society, the tax code is very simple and based on the IQ of each citizen. In such a settled society, the smarter persons, i.e. with higher IQ's, make more money. How they make it, is a private personal matter, and none of the government's business.

In using this basic premise, the writer can pick different characters and tell the reader how well this system works (or doesn't). For instance, an autistic citizen may have a high IQ, and large IRS bill, but cannot pay it because he is not able to do normal work. Others may flourish, as they cherish their privacy, without the government knowing every facet of their lives.

Planet of Super Giants

Astronauts find an alternative planet to Earth, which had been devastated by global warming and warring. They arrive at a lush new planet, named Ergo, where refugees from Earth can colonize. One problem: The planet is inhabited by huge giants. They are so big, that the humans are equivalent to bedbugs, when they lived on Planet Earth. The giants' body hairs are larger than the Sequoia trees on Earth. As Ergo got populated with humans, many found shelter inside the giants' super homes. Some humans even lived in the hair forests on the bodies of these huge creatures. To the humans living in the hair jungle of a sleeping giant, it would be a long arduous journey from his chest's hair jungle, towards the pubic hair jungle, and finally off the body to go outside the house, if the weather permited.

There's lots of room for a writer's imagination as to how these two different creatures would share this same planet, without the giants noticing the humans, or being aggravated by them, the way humans got bugged by, well, say bugs!

Baseball on Commission

In this futuristic world, baseball players are not salaried. They play strictly on achievement, call it 'commission'. One pay schedule can look like this:

Homerun--$1,000 each;
Catch--$50 each;
Triple Play--$500; and so forth.

Based on this plot line, the writer can pick interesting characters, and describe how they interact with coaches and management. How they resolve disputes. The competition could be savage. For instance, a fly ball could attract 3 fielders pushing each other away from the ball, so that the one catching it can earn some income.

A similar scenario can be made up for basketball, football, soccer, etc.

Explosive TV Set

A super secret terrorist organization infiltrates a TV manufacturing operation, and plant an explosive in each targeted set. When the consumer uses the TV set at home, and presses the remote for a specific channel, perhaps anti-terrorism channel, the planted explosive, hidden inside the TV set explodes with a violent force that kills everyone in the room.

This theme lends itself to great suspense, with the author choosing the right characters in a well crafted story line. For instance, this being a new method by the terrorists, the authorities may not suspect terrorism; that it is merely poorly made TV sets overheating and exploding. So a TV recall order can go out to correct any defect. Then the plot gets thicker, as they say, with the writer ushering the story to a perhaps unexpected and interesting conclusion.

Silencer

A scientist is driven almost to nuts by all the loud voices around him. He invents a TV-style sound remote, but for people. A special ray hits a person's vocal chords, and his/her voice is silenced, even while the lips continue to flap words, which are no longer heard.

Based on this theme, an author can create a story and apply it in real life. The characters can be his family members, business associates, or the public in parks, zoos, etc. The inventor can also try it on rowdy animals, noisy night crickets, or recurring maddening cicadas.

Casino Car Hijacked

Beautiful car is on display in the casino waiting for the lucky winner. Late one night, when there is no one around this car, a gambling auto mechanic, who is also an impatient loser, gets in the car, shorts the ignition, turns the engine on, and drives it out of the casino, onto the highway and home, if no one noticed him; or into hiding, if any witness saw enough to find him.

In this story line, the writer can create an attractive and mysterious casino atmosphere, with contrasting characters rubbing shoulders to play slot machines or gamble at tables. There would good suspense casing the area around the prize car, waiting for the right moment to steal the valuable vehicle. The author could develop a plot that deals with the situation after the thief takes off with the automobile; does he take it home? What does his wife (or mother) react?

Printed in the United States
By Bookmasters